UNEXPECTED TWiST

A Modern Retelling of Oliver Twist

Scholastic Children's Books
An imprint of Scholastic Ltd
Euston House, 24 Eversholt Street, London, NW1 1DB, UK
Registered office: Westfield Road, Southam, Warwickshire, CV47 0RA
SCHOLASTIC and associated logos are trademarks and/or
registered trademarks of Scholastic Inc.

First published in the UK by Scholastic Ltd, 2018

Text copyright © Michael Rosen, 2018
Illustrations copyright © Tony Ross, 2018

The right of Michael Rosen and Tony Ross to be identified as the author
and illustrator of this work has been asserted by them.

Trade ISBN 978 1407 18856 0

Printed by CPI Group (UK) Ltd, Croydon, CR0 4YY
Papers used by Scholastic Children's Books are made
from wood grown in sustainable forests.

1 3 5 7 9 10 8 6 4 2

www.scholastic.co.uk

UNEXPECTED TWiST

Michael Rosen

Illustrated by
Tony Ross

SCHOLASTIC

Chapter 1

"Hands up, who can remember the day they were born?" Miss Cavani looked round the class just as she always did when asking a searching question, her eyes and eyebrows full of hope that there would be at least one person in the room who could answer. As it was early in the day, she was at her breeziest best, and she scanned the room. Class X10 were not expecting this particular question, or anything like it, though they were getting used to the way Miss

Cavani asked questions you couldn't possibly predict.

Rory put his hand up.

"Really? I mean ... really?" Miss Cavani said to him.

By now, the room had started to shuffle and snigger, a few smiles flickered to and fro. The general view was that of course you can't remember the day you're born, and Rory, hah! Well, yeah, Rory would say something like that.

"Yeah, but you don't remember," Crayton said, in his usual very direct way.

"Wait your turn, please, Crayton." Miss Cavani dived into the chat between Rory and Crayton like an agile referee.

"Yeah, but he doesn't, Miss," said Crayton.

Miss Cavani's look hovered for a moment as she wondered if it was a good idea to put Crayton on a "warning" or carry on with her plan to interest Class X10 in birth. She decided to carry on and her gaze fixed again on Rory.

"Well, Rory?"

Rory was now flummoxed and flustered; he muttered something and then swallowed it before it got any further than his lips. Crayton had got him right. No one remembers the day they were born and the only reason he had put his hand up was for the usual reason he put his hand up: to say something – anything – that would secure for him a moment of approval from Miss Cavani. Why not? Almost everyone thought it felt good to get approval from Miss Cavani.

Next to Rory, Harry knew the deal here and he *could* choose to join the others grinning and whispering behind their hands, and he could also take part in the mockery that would erupt when Rory would say, "Well ... er ... actually ... no, I ... er ... can't ... the thing is ... I mean..." Or, if he paused a moment to think about it, Harry could think quickly and save him.

Harry put his hand up.

"Yes?" said Miss Cavani.

"We don't actually remember the day we were born, but, I mean, there are films where babies are born and anyway, your parents always tell stuff about how the doctor got your dad's name wrong or a light bulb blew, so even if you don't remember, you kind of know about it anyway."

"Yeah," said Rory. And Harry heard the smallest of breaths coming from Rory: at that, Harry knew he had pulled Rory out of the fire. He glanced at Miss Cavani and Harry knew that Miss Cavani had seen what Harry had done there. Hey, it was as good as a "well done!" without a word being spoken.

The rest of the class sank back. Harry had cheated them of a small moment when they could feel superior to someone in the endless jostle of school life. A car revved outside and the voice of an angry van man or cabbie filtered into the room. Serena pushed a note towards Rasheda. Miss Cavani missed it. Sometimes even Miss Cavani missed stuff.

She missed it because she was glancing down at her lesson plan. The discussion about "birth" was not going according to the plan, but Miss Cavani was not just a teacher-teacher, she had also spent time in some kind of theatre – something that was a source of endless gossip, laughter and mystery in the school. The class had an idea that this "theatre" thing was what made her different – particularly in the way that it seemed to have given her the power to suddenly change course, switch tack, improvise. She dropped the plan.

"Stories! Harry tells us that our parents tell stories about the day we were born. True? Untrue?"

She clapped her hands. "Into your Talk Groups, and tell each other what stories your parents – or anyone, maybe not your parents – have told you about the day you were born. Go!"

The room came alive, as chairs were lugged round, people turned towards each other, the noise level rose and soon, out came stories of dads fainting, the eggs of a pigeon on the window sill outside the birthing room hatching at the same time as the birth, an emergency birth on a train, a stand-up row about naming the baby, a father who had never been seen since, a terrible moment when someone stopped breathing – was it the baby or the mother? – and on and on. If nothing else, this was a bit of a laugh. Did Harry make up that stuff about being born in a Greek restaurant?

Miss Cavani clapped her hands again.

"And you're here! Just think, you might not have made it. Maybe some of you know sad, sad, sad stories of births that went wrong. But here's another thought: for you to be here now, thousands of people all over the world, living before you, had to have survived that moment of coming into the world."

A question mark raced round the class. What did she mean? Miss Cavani sensed it.

"Your parents were born. Their parents, and their parents, and their parents, and their parents and their parents going back and back and back hundreds and thousands of years. All born. All survived. And many, many times in that long line, people linked to you were within a breath of being snuffed out and ending the line."

This was too uncomfortable for Désol'é, who began to draw jagged lines on the page in front of

her. Rasheda passed a note back to Serena. This time Miss Cavani spotted it but chose to ignore it.

"Imagine, over a hundred and fifty years ago, in this country, and someone in your line was really, really, really poor. Too poor to have a house, a home, a room, or even a shed to live in. No place of their own. They had to live in the …"

Here Miss Cavani did her raised eyebrow thing, hoping yet again that someone would finish her sentence.

"… in the …?"

"Odeon."

It was Sunil. The Odeon cinema. He was quick. He loved to wait for gaps when people were talking and dive in with the unexpected. Sometimes it worked; sometimes it didn't. This one did. He got the laughs he was looking for. Nearly everyone liked the idea his gag conjured up of people, long before films were invented, who were so poor that they somehow miraculously ended up in a cinema from the future, kipping under the seats and living off popcorn.

A frown of irritation sprouted between Miss Cavani's eyes. Sunil had washed away a mood that had focussed just where she had wanted it: on coming into the world.

"Oh, yes, of course, Sunil," she said, "or what about the airport? There were airports on every street corner a hundred and fifty years ago, weren't there? Poor people used to live in the departure lounges."

Coming from some teachers, this kind of put-down was loathed, but somehow with Miss Cavani, everyone rather liked these improvisations.

Rasheda turned to Serena, nodded and whispered, "Sarky!"

Miss Cavani heard it. "Sarky?" she asked. "Sarky? Hold that thought."

Another of Miss Cavani's sayings, like you could "hold" a thought! Where? How? What in? Or, her other one: where she said how "thinking on your feet" was great, as if thinking sitting down was rubbish.

"Let's just sort this out, X10. I didn't have in

mind the Odeon cinema; I didn't have in mind the airport. But as we've been doing a bit of weird time-travelling here, I'm sending you and your parents to the workhouse. Yes, the workhouse. You'll love it. It's like a prison for people who haven't done anything wrong. Apart from being poor. And we all know how bad and evil it is to be poor..."

Rasheda turned to Serena again. They had promised each other they would keep count of the number of the times Miss Cavani did this sort of thing. Serena again mouthed, "Sarky!"

Miss Cavani caught it.

"Sarky? I tell you what, if you think I'm sarky, wait till you see someone being really sarky – sarcastic, that is."

Miss Cavani stopped mid-flow.

"Or perhaps you'll think it's ironic rather than sarcastic. I wonder. Hmmm. Serena, you can be our expert on such things; start us off, please."

At that, Serena, looked down at the page in front of her, paused while a plane went over, and started to read:

Although being born in a workhouse is not the most fortunate and enviable circumstance that can possibly befall a human being, in this particular instance, it was the best thing for Oliver Twist that could have occurred. The fact is, that there was considerable difficulty in getting Oliver to breathe - a troublesome practice, but one that is necessary to our easy existence - and for some time he lay gasping on a little flock mattress, poised between this world and the next. Now, if, during this brief period, Oliver had been surrounded by careful grandmothers, anxious aunts, experienced nurses, and doctors of profound wisdom, he would inevitably have been killed in no time. There being nobody by, however, but a pauper old woman, who was rendered rather misty by beer, and a parish surgeon who did such matters by contract; Oliver and Nature fought out the point between them. The result was, that, after a few struggles, Oliver breathed, sneezed, and proceeded to set up as loud a cry as could reasonably have been expected from a male infant who had not been possessed of a voice for much longer than three minutes and a quarter.

There was a rattling, riddling sound from the door handle of the classroom door, followed by the door itself opening.

Serena stopped.

Everyone looked towards the door. It was Mrs Buthelezi and a girl who was around the same age as the students in the class. She was small and wiry but not weak-looking. Far from it. With her strong, bright eyes, she wasn't afraid of looking at the class, which she did without smiling. She looked up at Mrs Buthelezi who was the tallest person in the room – and she knew it. No one had a real handle on what

Mrs Buthelezi's actual job was, but she was the one who came to find you if your dad had suddenly had to go into hospital. And she was in charge of forms. If you had to fill in a form, Mrs Buthelezi had the form. Any form, any size. Today, Mrs Buthelezi's job was to bring in a girl. And a form. She smiled at the girl and the girl looked from Mrs Buthelezi's face to Miss Cavani's face and then towards the class. Mrs Buthelezi smiled. She was good at smiling.

Mrs Buthelezi handed Miss Cavani the form, nodded, waved very quickly in Harry's direction for some reason, and left.

Miss Cavani put her arm out towards the girl in a welcoming way, glanced at the form and said, "Shona!"

"All alone-a!" whispered Sunil. There he was again. In the gap. This time with one of his rhymes. He once told Crayton that one day he would be, like, the best ever at freestyling.

"Now then," said Miss Cavani, doing her best to keep everything together (which was why she clasped and unclasped her hands), "this is Shona. Shona is new to the school, and she's in this class. It can't be easy coming into a new school and a new class, so let's show our appreciation that Shona's overcome this."

Miss Cavani started to clap and everyone joined in.

It seemed a bit over the top. It gave the class time to take in more of what Shona looked like and what she was wearing. The style and clothes experts – like Crayton or Serena – picked up on how her trainers were cracked and not only was she still wearing the uniform of the school she had come from but also that the uniform itself was ready for the bin: like the cloth itself was tired. Was there something that Miss Cavani wasn't saying about Shona?

"Shona, will you please sit down over there, where there's that spare place by Harry? We're reading a book called *Oliver Twist*. Harry, can you tell Shona what's happened so far?"

Harry looked at the page and said, without looking at Shona, "There's a boy called Oliver Twist, who's been born. And I think an old woman is drunk. And there's some sort of a joke going on where the person who's written this story tells it in really grand language like it's properly posh people. But it's not."

Crayton nudged Harry: "It's in a workhouse."

"Right, it really isn't posh at all. It's in a workhouse," Harry added. "A workhouse is—"

"I know what a workhouse is," said Shona.

"Do you? That's good," said Miss Cavani, "then we'll carry on. Serena, as you were."

And Serena carried on...

As Oliver gave this first proof of the free and proper action of his lungs, the patchwork coverlet that had been carelessly flung over the iron bedstead rustled; the pale face of a young woman was raised feebly from the pillow, and a faint voice imperfectly articulated the words, "Let me see the child, and die."

The surgeon had been sitting with his face turned towards the fire: giving the palms of his hands a warm and a rub alternately. As the young woman spoke, he rose, and advancing to the bed's head, said, with more kindness than might have been expected of him:

"Oh, you must not talk about dying yet."

"Lor bless her dear heart, no!" interposed the nurse, hastily depositing in her pocket a green glass bottle, the contents of which she had been tasting in a corner with evident satisfaction.

The surgeon deposited the child in her arms. She imprinted her cold white lips passionately on its forehead, passed her hands over her face, gazed wildly round, shuddered, fell back - and died.

"It's all over, Mrs Thingummy!" said the surgeon at last.

"Ah, poor dear, so it is!" said the nurse, picking up the cork of the green bottle, which had fallen out on the pillow, as she stooped to take up the child. "Poor dear!"

"You needn't bother fetching me if the child cries, nurse," said the surgeon, putting on his gloves with great deliberation. "It's very likely it will be troublesome. Give it a little gruel if it is." He put on his hat, and, pausing by the bedside on his way to the door, added, "She was a good-looking girl, too; where did she come from?"

"She was brought here last night," replied the old woman, "She was found lying in the street. She had walked some distance, for her shoes were worn to pieces; but where she came from, or where she was going to, nobody knows."

The surgeon leaned over the body, and raised the left hand. "The old story," he said, shaking his head: "no wedding ring, I see. Ah! Goodnight!"

The medical gentleman walked away to dinner; and the nurse, having once more applied herself to the green bottle, sat down on a low chair before the fire, and proceeded to dress the infant.

What an excellent example of the power of dress, young Oliver Twist was! Wrapped in the blanket which had hitherto formed his only covering, he might have been the child of a nobleman or a beggar; it would have been hard for the haughtiest stranger to have guessed his proper station in society. But now that he was enveloped in old calico robes that had grown yellow in service, he was badged and ticketed, and fell into his place at once - a parish child - the orphan of a workhouse - the humble, half-starved drudge - to be cuffed and buffeted through the world - despised by all, and pitied by none.

Oliver cried lustily. If he could have known that he was an orphan, left to the tender mercies of church wardens and overseers, perhaps he would have cried the louder.

The bell for the end of the lesson rang just at the point where it said, "Oliver cried lustily" so that the thought of a baby crying and a bell ringing merged into each other. Miss Cavani indicated with her hand and fierce eyes that she wanted everyone to stay exactly where they were until Serena reached the end of the passage.

Then, when Serena pronounced the last words, Miss Cavani held up her hand and said, "Thank you, Serena. Thank you, Class X10. Remember, Oliver is left to the mercies of church wardens and overseers, but you – yes, you! – are left to the mercies of me and the rest of the staff. You'll have to decide who has the easier life, you or Oliver. Off you go!"

In the jumble of chairs on the floor, pencil cases

closing, bags being gathered, Désol'é edged towards Shona. What Miss Cavani said about being left to the mercies of others might have echoed in Shona's mind as Désol'é said to her, "There's, like, a new serve-yourself cafeteria thing. Come?"

Shona nodded.

Chapter 2

The next day, Shona rushed down the corridor – was it left at the end or right? And was it room 4.09 or 4.08? It seemed as if the whole school was squeezing down the corridor in the opposite direction and she was fighting them to get through. As she pushed against them, they pushed against her. Did someone try to grab her bag, or did it just get caught up in the flow for a moment?

She reached room 4.09 and looked in. It was empty. Odd! She thought she was late. Or was she in the wrong room? She felt herself breathing. The last thing she wanted was to get into trouble so soon after coming to this school. *It isn't fair,* she thought, that she had to leave the old one anyway. One day, you're in a place and the next, you have to move. She remembered everyone had been talking for ages about "benefits" and she knew only too well that Dad was "on benefits". The first time she heard it, she thought it sounded kind of sweet, a little bit extra. But now she was a bit older, she was getting it that Dad and her needed the "benefit" to live off. And right now they said they were "stopping it". *Which means,* Shona thought to herself, *we've got to move.*

As she rushed towards the door, Harry walked in. He nodded.

Shona nodded back. "Is it in here?" she asked.

"What?" Harry replied.

"English," Shona said. "It said on the thingy that because of the flooding in North Block, it was over here."

"Yep," said Harry.

Harry knew and Shona knew that they were supposed to be sitting next to each other, but it felt really awkward to sit down next to each other in an empty room. Just the two of them. So Harry stood in the middle of the room, feeling more awkward than if he had gone to sit down.

Shona seemed less bothered than him and said, "Is it OK? This school?"

"Yeah," said Harry in as unenthusiastic voice as he could manage. "Yeah, OK. You know."

Shona looked straight at him in a way that Harry found quite tricky. "Teachers OK?" Shona asked. He noticed her eyes.

"Oh yeah. They're OK," Harry said, "one or two are … you know…"

A thought came into Shona's head about teachers. You're in school with them all day, and you think you know them, but behind the scenes they're saying and doing loads of stuff you never know about. You don't even know what they say to each other when they go to meetings.

The others started to come into the room with stories about how they got turned away from North Block: Sunil and Crayton got stopped by Mr Grimble on the Causeway, and Désol'é dropped her French book in the pond. (It was OK; the plastic cover kept it mostly dry before she fished it out again.)

A good few minutes after everyone had arrived, Miss Cavani dashed in, stuffing her phone into her bag. She was furious. She had been told that the class was in room 3.05 and had gone there instead, she explained. No matter. She was here now. She pushed back the hair on the sides of her head and tightened her lips.

Was she really that furious about room 3.05, or was it something she had just heard on her phone?

"Sorry, X10, got caught in a meeting. Just ought to pass this on to you: from now on, the school can't provide food on the premises for students, apart from for teachers. As you are not allowed off the premises during lunchtime, and you're not allowed to bring any food on to the premises, it's going to be – how shall I put it? – a long day."

There was an immediate outbreak of indignant noise. It was a roar of outrage.

Miss Cavani held up her hand and demanded silence. "We'll discuss this later. In the meantime, let's read on. This time, let's break it up a little. Shona, would you read the narration?"

Shona anxiously shook her head.

"Rory?"

Rory nodded.

"So this narrator – "Charles Dickens", we can call him, if you like – is Rory; Rasheda, you read Mrs Mann; Crayton, please read Mr Bumble; and Désol'é, you can read Oliver Twist."

The indignant noise about food did subside when Miss Cavani had asked for silence, but it simmered along through the reading.

CLASS X10 READING COMPREHENSION

The parish authorities sent Oliver to a branch workhouse some three miles off, where twenty or thirty other juvenile offenders against the poor laws rolled about the floor all day, without the inconvenience of too much food or too much clothing, under the parental superintendence of an elderly female, who received sevenpence-halfpenny per small head per week. The elderly female was a woman of wisdom and experience; she knew what was good for children; and she had a very accurate idea of what was good for herself. So, she appropriated the greater part of the weekly allowance to her own use, and consigned the children to even less than was originally provided for them. .

It cannot be expected that this system of farming would produce any very extraordinary or luxuriant crop. Oliver Twist's ninth birthday found him a pale, thin child, and decidedly small. But nature or inheritance had implanted a good sturdy spirit in Oliver's breast. It had had plenty of room to expand, thanks to his spare diet. He was keeping his birthday in the coal cellar with a select party of two other young gentleman, who, after participating with him in receiving a sound thrashing, had been locked up for atrociously presuming to be hungry, when Mrs Mann, the good lady of the house, was unexpectedly startled by the sight of Mr Bumble, the beadle, striving to undo the wicket of the garden gate.

"Goodness gracious! Is that you, Mr Bumble, sir?" said Mrs Mann, thrusting her head out of the window in well-affected ecstasies of joy. "(Susan, take Oliver and them two brats upstairs, and wash 'em directly.) - My heart alive! Mr Bumble, how glad I am to see you, surely!"

Now, Mr Bumble was a fat man, and a bad-tempered one; so, instead of responding to this open-hearted salutation in a kindred spirit, he gave the little wicket a tremendous shake, and then bestowed upon it a kick which could have emanated from no leg but a beadle's.

"Lor, only think," said Mrs Mann, running out - for the three boys had been removed by this time - "only think of that! That I should have forgotten that the gate was bolted on the inside, on account of them dear children! Walk in, sir; walk in, pray, Mr Bumble, do, sir."

"Lead the way in, Mrs Mann, for I come

on business, and have something to say."
Mrs Mann ushered the beadle into a small parlour with a brick floor; placed a seat for him; and officiously deposited his cocked hat and cane on the table before him.

"Now don't you be offended at what I'm a going to say," observed Mrs Mann with captivating sweetness. "You've had a long walk, you know, or I wouldn't mention it. Now, will you take a little drop of somethink, Mr Bumble?"

"Not a drop. Not a drop," said Mr Bumble, waving his right hand in a dignified, but placid manner.

"I think you will," said Mrs Mann, who had noticed the tone of the refusal, and the gesture that had accompanied it. "Just a leetle drop, with a little cold water, and a lump of sugar."

Mr Bumble coughed.

"Now, just a leetle drop," said Mrs Mann persuasively.

"What is it?" inquired the beadle.

"Why, it's what I'm obliged to keep a little of in the house, to put into the blessed infants' Daffy, when they ain't well, Mr Bumble," replied Mrs Mann as she opened a corner cupboard, and took down a bottle and glass. "It's gin. I'll not deceive you, Mr B. It's gin."

"Do you give the children Daffy, Mrs Mann?" inquired Bumble, following with his eyes the interesting process of mixing.

"Ah, bless 'em, that I do, dear as it is," replied the nurse. "I couldn't see 'em suffer before my very eyes, you know, sir."

"No," said Mr Bumble approvingly, "no, you could not. You are a humane woman, Mrs Mann." (Here she set down the glass.) "I shall take an early opportunity of mentioning it to the board, Mrs Mann." (He drew it towards him.) "You feel as a mother, Mrs Mann." (He stirred the gin and water.) "I drink your

The beadle drew himself up with great pride, and said, "I inwented it."

"You, Mr Bumble!"

"I, Mrs Mann. We name our fondlings in alphabetical order. The last was a S - Swubble, I named him. This was a T - Twist, I named him. The next one comes will be Unwin, and the next Vilkins. I have got names ready made to the end of the alphabet, and all the way through it again, when we come to Z."

"Why, you're quite a literary character, sir!" said Mrs Mann.

"Well, well," said the beadle, evidently gratified with the compliment; "perhaps I may be. Perhaps I may be, Mrs Mann." He finished the gin and water, and added, "Oliver being now too old to remain here, the board have determined to have him back into the workhouse. I have come out myself to take him there. So let me see him at once."

"I'll fetch him directly," said Mrs Mann, leaving the room for that purpose. Oliver, having had by this time as much of the outer coat of dirt which encrusted his face and hands removed, as could be scrubbed off in one washing, was led into the room.

"Make a bow to the gentleman, Oliver," said Mrs Mann.

Oliver made a bow, which was divided between the beadle on the chair, and the hat on the table.

"Will you go along with me, Oliver?" said Mr Bumble, in a majestic voice.

Oliver was about to say that he would go along with anybody with great readiness, when, glancing upward, he caught sight of Mrs Mann, who had got behind the beadle's chair, and was shaking her fist at him with a furious expression. He took the hint at once, for the fist had been too often impressed upon his body not to be deeply impressed upon his recollection.

"Will she go with me?" inquired poor Oliver.

"No, she can't," replied Mr Bumble. "But she'll come and see you sometimes."

This was no very great consolation to the child. Young as he was, however, he had sense enough to make a show of feeling great regret at going away. It was no very difficult matter for the boy to call tears into his eyes. Hunger and recent abuse are great assistants if you want to cry; and Oliver cried very naturally indeed. Mrs Mann gave him a thousand embraces, and what Oliver wanted a great deal more: a piece of bread and butter, so he would not seem too hungry when he got to the workhouse. With the slice of bread in his hand, and the little brown-cloth parish cap on his head, Oliver was then led away by Mr Bumble from the wretched home where one kind word or look had never lighted the gloom of his infant years. And yet he burst into an agony of childish grief, as the cottage gate closed after him. Wretched as were the little companions in misery he was leaving behind, they were the only friends he had ever known; and a sense of his loneliness in the great wide world sank into the child's heart for the first time.

Sunil sat back. "Miss. About this thing and the food in school."

"Yes, Sunil?" Miss Cavani said, with one eyebrow slightly raised.

"Is it true? Or did you make that up?"

A buzz went round the room. Though Miss Cavani liked students to be "forthright", as she put it, most knew not to confront her quite as directly as Sunil just had.

Miss Cavani glanced at her watch. "We've got two minutes left. In your Talk Groups. Was Miss Cavani telling the truth? Or did she make that up about the food in school? If it's true, fine. If I made it up, why? Anything to do with *Oliver Twist*, perhaps..?" And up went the Cavani eyebrow in a question-mark curve.

Everyone had something to say. If they had been asked that question straight after Miss Cavani had told them that they wouldn't be allowed to eat during the school day, while the teachers could, they would almost all have said she had been telling the truth. But now ... but now? It was bogus, wasn't it? It was one of her "think about it" things that connected up in some Miss-Cavani-kind-of-a-way with what they were supposed to be working on.

She clapped her hands. "I'll take a vote. All those in favour of Miss Cavani telling the truth, raise your hand."

Two people raised their hands.

"All those in favour of Miss Cavani having made it all up, raise your hand."

It was everyone else.

The bell went and Miss Cavani swept out, to cries of "Well, which is it, Miss?"

"Is it true, Miss?"

"If it's not true, why did you say it, Miss?"

At the end of school, Shona gathered her stuff together, and felt a knot form in her stomach at the thought of going back to the flat they were moving out of. Dad had started to pack stuff into bags, he was going on about the "elex" – the electricity – as

Shona knew only too well as he was always on at her to switch off the lights as it "used up the juice", another of his electricity words. It wasn't home any more. *Best stay away for a bit*, she thought. She felt the key on the string round her neck. She could get in when she felt like it. Which she didn't feel like. *I know*, she thought, *I'll go and see Nan.*

In her mind's eye, she saw Nan standing at her stall at the market. Maybe she'd ask Shona to open up some boxes, or go fetch her a cup of tea. Maybe even serve the punters. She could do homework later on, sometime.

Somewhere.

Yes, that's what she'd do. Go see Nan.

As she turned left at the school gates, to head towards the high street, she saw Désol'é on the other side of the road. Her face was down and she held a paper hankie up by her nose. It looked as if she was crying.

Shona strolled up to the market stall, just as Nan was being handed a box by a large man. Nan quickly shoved it under the stall and then, the moment the two caught sight of Shona, the man slipped away into the stream of people filling the road and Nan put on the look of someone doing nothing.

"Not packing up your stuff ready for the move?" Nan asked Shona a bit sharply.

"No," said Shona.

"You're looking perky," Nan said, even though Shona felt just the opposite.

"Can I help you for a bit?" Shona asked

"That'd be lovely, angel, but I tell you, I'll die if I don't get a cup a tea in me," said Nan and handed Shona some money.

Shona knew just what to do: the Kettle Caff was, very conveniently, only a few steps from Nan's stall. Shona loved it in there, the smell of chips and kebabs and hot pitta bread mingling in her nose.

Zeynep knew who Shona was, and who the tea was for. She smiled and poured it into a paper cup, snapped on the lid, put a cardboard collar round it to stop it burning Shona's hand, and passed it to her.

Shona tried to give Zeynep the money, but she waved it away. Shona was confused: she had never done that before.

Zeynep moved Shona away. She seemed upset. It seemed like Zeynep knew something, or was saying something … and yet wasn't.

Back at the stall, Shona handed over the hot tea, followed by the money.

"What's this?" said Nan, looking at the money.

"Zeynep wouldn't take it."

Nan looked away and muttered, "She's being kind."

"Oh, yes," Shona said, not understanding what was going on.

"I might as well tell you. I've been up the hospital, and this time it's serious."

Shona put her hand on Nan's arm, and Nan gave her a small smile in return. Nan had been struggling for a while now with something bad – Shona wasn't exactly sure what, and this wasn't the first time things had got serious. There had been talk of "it coming back". Shona kept her hand on Nan's arm, and Nan seemed to like it being there.

Shona wondered whether giving Nan a cup of tea for nothing could make things any better for Nan. But, then, she had known for as long as she had known anything, round Nan's stall a lot of things happened this way: "I'll do you a favour if you do me a favour" or, "I won't say anything about that, if you don't say anything about the other thing…", all done with a nod here and a "Don't ask!" there.

Chapter 3

How much time do we spend in corridors? Shona wondered.

She was walking along the upper corridor in North Block, having already run down the Causeway – a path that ran between two slightly smelly ponds – through the Passage, and down the short tunnel under the track to the East Field, when a policewoman in a high-vis jacket stepped to one side to let her through. She smiled at Shona, and Shona came out of the tunnel thinking, *I'm getting the hang of all these directions and distances.* On past the Unit – whatever that was – and just as she was thinking that she had done OK – or better than OK – to have done this, a loud voice caught up with her.

"Who are you?"

Shona turned.

It was a vigorous young teacher who Shona noticed must have cut himself shaving that morning. As Shona hadn't replied in less than half of a second, he asked the same question, but more loudly: "Who ARE you?"

Shona felt herself shrink, and shrinking wasn't very helpful in getting her to speak. So, she just stood in front of the man with the shaving cut.

"Where's your lanyard?" he shouted again.

The lanyard! Mrs Buthelezi had said that the machine that did the photo (or was it the card? or, come to think of it, was it the ribbon?) for the identity lanyard that everyone had to wear was broken. But it didn't matter – or so Mrs Buthelezi said – because Mrs Buthelezi had sent round a memo saying that Shona wouldn't be wearing a lanyard while the lanyard machine was broken.

Somehow or another that piece of information had not reached the man who had cut himself shaving.

"All students must wear lanyards at all times," he said to Shona.

She looked at him.

He repeated what he had just said: "All students must wear lanyards at ALL times!" – as if saying "ALL" a bit louder would make it much clearer.

Shona went on looking at him and now focussed on the scab on his right cheek where his razor had cut his skin. It was slightly moist, as if something inside his cheek was trying to get out.

"I don't recognize you," the man went on.

Still Shona said nothing. What was there to say? He was just blurting things at her and not waiting to see if there were reasons for stuff. Anyway, he wouldn't listen if she did give reasons. "You had better come with me to my office," he said.

Shona knew this was wrong. The reason why

she was in the upper corridor of North Block was that she had to get to a maths lesson which was not actually going to be a lesson, but had been flagged up as a maths test. And whatever else was going on in their lives, the maths teacher, Mr Dur, had said they all had to do the test. Mr Dur had made this sound so important that everyone, especially Shona, felt that missing the test might well result in something like ten years in prison.

"I've got a maths test, with Mr Dur." Shona finally felt she had to say something.

"Well," said the man, so distracted by the way Shona kept looking at his shaving cut that he now brought his hand up to his face and cautiously touched the moist scab, "you can't do your maths test if you haven't got your lanyard."

Now, Shona didn't mean to be rude, but sometimes she said things in a direct way that others took to be rude. Perhaps it was the way she looked when she said it. She knew that anyone could do a maths test, and having a lanyard – or not having a lanyard – didn't really come into it. *You really could do a test without a lanyard*, Shona thought, so she said, "I can do the test without a lanyard."

The moment she said it, she knew it had come out wrong, but she didn't have the words to say how or that she hadn't meant it in a rude way. But it was too late.

"I'm giving you a D8," he said, his eyes fixed on her.

The only problem with this was that Shona hadn't been in the school long enough to know what a D8 was. She guessed it wasn't a present, but beyond that, what? An extra maths lesson? A spell in the lanyard factory making lanyards?

Just then, down the corridor came Mr Dur, a small, quick-moving man who always wore a suit that announced it was a suit because it had huge lapels. It felt as if things were going to get a whole lot worse. Mr Dur had made it clear that everyone was supposed to be in class before he arrived to hand out the test papers, yet here she was in the corridor. Not in class.

"Is this student supposed to be with you now?"

asked the man who had been so bothered about Shona's lack of lanyard.

Mr Dur looked closely at Shona and then said, "No."

Shona felt everything slipping away. Nothing was going right.

Shona could see that Lanyard Man was making himself a little bit taller, allowing himself a smile – and she knew that he had, after all, caught out someone who was trying to get round school without a lanyard and who was now obviously *a liar*. She could see from his look that he thought she was up to something sinister, and – look at him puffing himself up – he was on to it!

"Well, well, well," he said, "so, no maths test with Mr Dur. Your little story is falling apart."

Hearing "maths test with Mr Dur" seemed to flip a switch in Mr Dur's mind, and he looked back at Shona. In the great ocean of students' faces that ebbed and flowed through his brain, Shona's face had at first floated by; but now, triggered by "maths test with Mr Dur", it bobbed past on the top of the

Set 2P wave. Set 2P, the maths group that Shona had been put in because someone (who? why?) deep in the heart of the maths department had decided that she was at Set 2P level.

Shona now watched Mr Dur as he thought it through: the new student – Shona, yes! – the one that Yolanda Cavani had been talking about in the staff room.

But Lanyard Man was already pointing down the corridor towards some distant place where Shona figured she might be dumped and left for dead.

Mr Dur stepped forwards. "I'm sorry, it's not a 'no'. It's a 'yes'."

Lanyard Man put his head to one side. He liked things to go smoothly. It had been going smoothly. Now it wasn't going smoothly. "Mm?" he said in as aggressive a way as he could.

"She's with me," Mr Dur said.

This immediately posed a huge problem for Lanyard Man. He had stated quite clearly that it wasn't possible to do a maths test without a lanyard, and he had rumbled that Shona had lied about needing to be at some kind of maths test. Now the whole construction that he had built around this awful student was crumbling to dust.

Shona could see that Lanyard Man wanted to drag her down the corridor, while Mr Dur wanted to drag her towards the maths test. She was the rope in a tug of war. The two men glared at each other.

Mr Dur flicked his wrist and looked at his watch. "This is the Interim Level 7 Assessment," he said.

Whatever "Interim Level 7 Assessment" was, it acted like a magic spell. Lanyard Man took a step backwards, bent slightly towards Mr Dur, held out his arm as if he was a traffic cop letting the cars go through, said, "As you were," turned and headed off down the corridor.

Without saying anything further, but simply gesturing with his thumb, Mr Dur indicated to Shona that she should head towards the room that she had planned on going to sometime earlier. As she scampered along beside Mr Dur, she felt her bag slip out of her hand, and as it fell, her books, pencil case and Miss Cavani's homework fell on the floor. On the top was...

CLASS X10 READING COMPREHENSION

Oliver had not been within the walls of the workhouse a quarter of an hour, and had scarcely completed the demolition of a second slice of bread, when Mr Bumble told him it was a board night, informing him that the board had said Oliver was to appear before it forthwith.

Not having a very clearly defined notion of what a board was, Oliver was rather astounded by this intelligence, and was not quite certain whether he ought to laugh or cry. He had no time to think about the matter, however, for Mr Bumble gave him a tap on the head with his cane, to wake him up; and another on the back to make him lively; and bidding him to follow, conducted him into a large whitewashed room, where eight or ten fat gentlemen were sitting round a table. At the top of the table, seated in an armchair rather higher than the rest, was a particularly fat gentleman with a very round, red face.

"Bow to the board," said Bumble. Oliver brushed away two or three tears that were lingering in his eyes; and seeing no board

but the table, fortunately bowed to that.

"What's your name, boy?" said the gentleman in the high chair.

Oliver was frightened at the sight of so many gentlemen, which made him tremble, and the beadle gave him another tap behind, which made him cry. These two causes made him answer in a very low and hesitating voice, whereupon a gentleman in a white waistcoat said he was a fool. Which was a capital way of raising his spirits, and putting him quite at his ease.

"Boy," said the gentleman in the high chair, "listen to me. You know you're an orphan, I suppose?"

"What's that, sir?" inquired poor Oliver.

"The boy is a fool - I thought he was," said the gentleman in the white waistcoat.

"Hush!" said the gentleman who had spoken first. "You know you've got no father or mother, and that you were brought up by the parish, don't you?"

"Yes, sir," replied Oliver, weeping bitterly.

"What are you crying for?" inquired the gentleman in the white waistcoat. And to be sure it was very extraordinary. What could the boy be crying for?

"I hope you say your prayers every night," said another gentleman in a gruff voice; "and pray for the people who feed you, and take care of you - like a Christian."

"Yes, sir," stammered the boy.

"Well! You have come here to be educated, and taught a useful trade," said the red-faced gentleman in the high chair.

"So you'll begin to pick oakum - that's pulling old ship's rope apart so that it can be re-used - tomorrow morning at six o'clock," added the surly one in the white waistcoat.

Oliver bowed low by the direction of the beadle, and was then hurried away to a large ward; where, on a rough, hard bed, he sobbed himself to sleep. What a novel poor people should have the alternative (for they would compel nobody, not they), of being starved by a gradual process in the workhouse, or by a quick one out of it. With this view, they contracted with the waterworks to lay on an unlimited supply of water; and with a corn factor to supply periodically small quantities of oatmeal; and issued three meals of thin gruel a day, with an onion twice a week, and half a roll on Sundays.

Chapter 4

Brackets. Shona remembered something to do with brackets. If you multiply something, the brackets disappear. In her mind's eye she saw her maths teacher at her previous school making brackets disappear. It seemed so simple when she did it, but here on the page in front of her, the brackets wouldn't disappear. They stayed right there, no matter what she did. She tried swapping one side over to another. And back again. Then dividing before multiplying.

She raised her head. Other people seemed to be speeding on.

Her mind wandered back to the corridor. Had she done something wrong? Yes, because Lanyard Man was angry with her. But what was it that she had done wrong? She couldn't answer that one, and her mind drifted towards the cut on his face. Cuts, *eurch*, knives, she shuddered in her mind. Once, when she was with Nan in the market she had seen someone whip a knife out. There was going to be bother. Shona felt cold thinking about it, and her mind wandered to what Nan had done at that moment. Strange, Nan seemed both to know what was going on and not know. Both at the same time. There were definitely things she couldn't figure out about Nan. Like how she'd talk of relatives that Shona had never seen. Who was that Lorraine in New York, who Nan always said "wasn't short of a penny or two" but Shona had never seen? And now her being ill. What was it she said? "This time it's serious", was it?

Into this stream of thought came that thing that Mr Dur had said, "Interim Level 7 Assessment". It was such a big deal that it had made Lanyard Man disappear. And here she was, trying to do Interim Level 7 Assessment. She thought back to the lesson when Mr Dur had said that they were going to do this test and how it would, as he said, "pretty well settle your fate for the rest of your time in this school". And there was something else Mr Dur had said about "your goose" being "cooked". What goose? And who was cooking it?

She looked back at the page. Was her life really

going to be decided by how she was doing in this test? The brackets that wouldn't disappear – were they going to cook her goose?

She looked at the next question. *Darren, Maria and Aysha have got some money and they're sharing it out.* Shona wondered why Darren, Maria and Aysha have got some money. Why has Lorraine in New York got money? *Darren had twice as much money as Maria, who's got half as much as Aysha.* That wasn't fair. Shona started drawing coins. This wasn't because she couldn't do the sum but because her old teacher had said that if you can't do it in your head, draw it.

Halfway through the right number of coins, Mr Dur walked past. He stopped next to Shona. He looked at the page filling up with little circles. All the way down to the bottom of the page. Mr Dur had explained that on this day of the Interim Level 7 Assessment he would not be a teacher, he would be an *invigilator*. It sounded cruel. *I will invigilate you! Then you'll be sorry!*

Mr Dur stood watching Shona.

Shona stopped. By now she was down at the bottom right-hand corner of the page. Shona moved the sheet of paper as if to make the paper tell her the answer.

"I think you need more," he said.

"I've got more paper here," Shona said, and she pointed at the next clean sheet of paper that was lying underneath the money page.

"No," said Mr Dur, "I meant money."

And he laughed.

Shona froze. Of course she needed more money. Dad's benefit had been stopped. That's why they were being moved from the flat to the room near the market. She felt her face flush red, and she imagined everyone looking at her. They would see that she was blushing and they would know that she and Dad had no money and that Mr Dur would know that and that all the teachers would know as well and they would think it was funny. All of them. Ha ha ha. Shona, the "poor" girl.

Her eyes couldn't see the page because they had filled with tears, but she wasn't going to let Mr Dur see that, so she kept her head down. She tried not to move.

Mr Dur went on standing right by her. "You need more money," he repeated, as if he wanted to shame her even more.

Now everyone had lifted their heads to see what was going on. They could see that some kind of stand-off was happening.

Shona did nothing.

Mr Dur said, "Four more. You need to draw four more coins." And he walked on.

The students nearby knew that he had helped her. Even in the midst of her rage that he had shamed her, Shona also had a vague sense that Mr Dur had helped her. And yet, she remembered he had said he wasn't teaching, he was invigilating. So had he broken the rules to be kind to her? She didn't ask for help. Did she look like someone who wanted help? *Hey you, Mr Dur,* she felt like saying, *I don't want you singling me out in front of everyone else. I don't want to be the one that you're kind to.*

She felt angry, confused, annoyed with herself

that at first she had got Mr Dur wrong. She was fed up with the test, and still mad at Lanyard Man who had got her in a state before this whole Interim Assess-test thing had happened.

She couldn't do any more of the test. She just stared at the page, gripping her pen till her knuckles stood out like chicken bones.

The class flowed out of the room with Shona being washed along in the current, and then, just as the stream washed past Mr Dur, she heard him say that thing about the goose being cooked again. He seemed to think it was funny.

Though most of Miss Cavani's English group weren't in this maths set, Désol'é was there, and as she was the only person Shona knew, she said to Désol'é, "What's a D8?"

"It's a detention," she said. "You have to go to 3.01 at the end of school and you sit there for an hour working out what's wrong with you."

"When?"

"Thursdays. You got one?"

"Yes."

"What for?"

"It was to do with my lanyard."

"You weren't wearing yours, right?" Désol'é glanced at Shona's neck, where the lanyard ribbon should have been.

"I said to a teacher that you don't need a lanyard to do a maths test."

"What?" Désol'é shrieked, "You said that? Are you crazy? You did OK just to get a D8, then! You could have got a D2 for that."

"D2?" Shona was lost in the jungle of school words.

"Right."

Shona wanted to know what a D2 was and how much worse than a D8 it was, because she was pretty sure that before long she'd be doing one of them too, but Désol'é had been swept up in the flow and was now ahead too.

At least, between now and the D8 there'd be Miss Cavani's lesson and that weird book they were reading. That was a bright spot up ahead.

The bowls never wanted washing. The boys polished them with their spoons till they shone again; and when they had performed this operation which never took very long, the spoons being nearly as large as the bowls, they would sit staring at the pot, with such eager eyes, as if they could have devoured the very bricks of which it was composed; employing themselves, meanwhile, in sucking their fingers most assiduously, with the view of catching up any stray splashes of gruel that might have been cast thereon. Boys have generally excellent appetites. Oliver Twist and his companions suffered the tortures of slow starvation for three months: at last they got so voracious and wild with hunger that one boy, who was tall for his age, and hadn't been used to that sort of thing for his father had kept a small cookshop, hinted darkly to his companions that unless he had another bowl of gruel per day, he was afraid he might some night happen to eat the boy who slept next him, who happened to be a weakly youth of tender age. He had a wild, hungry eye; and they believed him. A council was held; lots were cast who should walk up to the master after supper that evening, and ask for more; and it fell to Oliver Twist.

The evening arrived; the boys took their places. The master, in his cook's uniform, stationed himself at the pot; his pauper assistants arranged themselves behind him; the gruel was served out; and a long grace was said over the short commons. The gruel disappeared; the boys whispered to each other, and winked at Oliver; while his neighbours nudged him. Child as he was, he was desperate with hunger, and reckless with misery. He rose from the table; and advancing to the master, bowl and spoon in hand, said, somewhat alarmed at his own temerity:

"For more!" said Mr Limbkins. "Compose yourself, Bumble, and answer me distinctly. Do I understand that he asked for more, after he had eaten the supper allotted by the dietary?"

"He did, sir," replied Bumble.

An animated discussion took place. Oliver was ordered into instant confinement; and a bill was next morning pasted on the outside of the gate, offering a reward of five pounds to anybody who would take Oliver Twist off the hands of the parish. In other words, five pounds and Oliver Twist were offered to any man or woman who wanted an apprentice to any trade, business, or calling.

Chapter 5

The door to the flat was open, and Shona could see inside that there were cardboard boxes and the bags that Dad had been packing, now all over the floor.

"I thought you'd be back earlier," Dad said.

"So did I," Shona replied.

"Why weren't you?"

"Buses."

He grunted and looked down and into one of the bags, moved first one way, then another, picked something up, and put it down again. Shona looked at his shabby jumper, shabby trousers, shabby shoes. He was Mr Shabby. His face was beginning to take on the look of someone who was still in bed, something about how his cheeks and chin hardly moved when he talked and the skin looked pale and creased.

Behind this look, his mind was ticking over: he knew that sending her to this school ahead of the move was going to be a bit of a problem: two buses. Once they were in the new place, she'd be able to walk to school.

"You'd better know now, we haven't got as much space in the new place," he said.

"Why are we going there, then?" Shona asked.

"Because we've got no darned choice in the matter!" he shouted.

Why not, why not, why not? she said to herself. In one sense, she could answer her own question: it was because Dad couldn't work any more, couldn't earn any more, and yet he was losing his benefit – whatever that meant – and so they were moving – or was it they were being moved? – to a smaller place.

In another sense, she couldn't answer it: why were they in this fix, when others were not? There was never an answer to that one. Why weren't they like that relative in New York? Which reminded her of all those American kids on the Disney Channel who lived in great big white houses in the middle of huge gardens. Why did they have moms and dads and dogs and cars and she had, well, just Dad?

"Don't blooming just stand there. Go into your room; you've got less than half an hour to make up your mind what you're going to keep and what you're going to chuck. I've made it easy for you; you've got one box. Ron is coming over with his van, and we've got to fit the lot in there."

Shona did as she was told and stood in the middle of her room. Everything she had in the world was here, on the walls, on the shelves, under the bed, on the bed, on the little table, oh – the table itself, didn't Nan give that to her? Maybe she could ask Ron if they could squeeze that in somehow.

"Are you getting on with it?" Dad called from the other room. "I've got to sit down for a bit," he added.

When Shona went over to the "rec", she used to watch other dads running about kicking footballs and pushing their kids on swings, but Dad hadn't been able to manage that sort of thing for years.

Of course she used to watch the mums too.

There were always mums. Sitting together on benches, pushing buggies, wiping the corners of the mouths of toddlers, telling their kids to stop making a noise on the bus. What did it feel like to be told by a mum to not make so much noise on the bus? If she was "rattling on", as Dad put it, he used to just nudge her with his elbow. There were times when she had longed to be really yelled at by a mum. Nan was there when it happened. Just a few days after she was born.

Shona looked at the picture on the wall of the mum she never knew. There had been times, in the middle of the night, she had woken up and looked at the picture in the dark, and had imagined something so terrible that it made her shake. *If it happened because I*

was born, was it my fault? One day, when she was grown up, would the police turn up and say, *Shona, you're under arrest because, because...* Mum dying was her fault. The police would say that she, Shona was a... She couldn't say the word, couldn't even think it.

She would lie in bed, shaking, thinking about it, so terrified of the thought that she couldn't think, so terrified that she wouldn't ever tell anyone about it, ever, not even Nan, especially not Nan. After all, Mum was Nan's daughter. So, the secret that Shona thought, that she had done this terrible thing, she kept deep inside herself. But to keep it in there, she had to be careful and not give away too much.

"Have you started on that stuff, yet?" Dad called from the other room.

"Yeah, kind of," Shona replied and very, very slowly, she picked up an old broken mini-keyboard thing, plonked on one of the notes and put it on the rubbish pile. She had learned to play "She's Coming Round the Mountain" on that and had played it at her primary-school talent contest. Rubbish or not rubbish? Who cares either way? It's all rubbish, really.

She had once been in the house of a girl called Rhiannon at her primary school, and apart from all the lovely food and toys in her house, Shona had noticed that Rhiannon herself was all over the walls. The drawing she did when she was two, photos of her mounted on a big noticeboard: Rhiannon at the seaside, Rhiannon with Granny, Rhiannon with Granddad, Rhiannon with Granny P, Rhiannon with Grandpa, Rhiannon's swimming certificate. In the cupboard, there were shelves of Rhiannon toys like the shelves at school, and Rhiannon would say, "That's my Heeby Jeeby I had when I was five", or "That's my funny cowboy hat that Granny P brought back from Florida" and on and on and on. *I suppose Rhiannon still has all that stuff,* Shona thought. *And new stuff now, I bet ... the mobile, the tablet, the laptop. I bet she talks about box sets. And Netflix. I'll come away from here with Jimbo the elephant, my Jacqueline Wilson books, yes – maybe that keyboard thing, the photos of Mum, a few of those Playmobil things that aren't really Playmobil that Nan got me from the market.*

Nan! How ill is she? And that old, cold shaky dread thing started happening as Shona thought of the possibility that Nan was even more ill than she was letting on, so ill that, that – don't say the word … and maybe Zeynep knew all about it… *What will I have, then – apart from Dad? Just me. I'll have me. Yes, I'll have me.*

Later, Ron arrived and he trundled to and fro with the stuff they were taking, and the stuff they weren't taking he just chucked in the skip outside. Someone from the landlord's came over and said that they would send the bill on.

Dad said under his breath, "Send it where you like, pal, I'm not paying."

"What bill?" Shona asked him.

"He says I owe him for the damage."

"What damage?"

"Oh, it doesn't matter. They charge you whether there's damage or not. One place I was in, they said the cooker was covered in some stuff that they couldn't get off and it took five women a whole week to get it off, so I was supposed to pay for that. Jokers."

Shona took it all in, heard it, understood some of it, didn't have a clue about some of it, remembered some of it, forgot some of it, while the rest just floated out into the misty evening air.

As Dad went slowly downstairs with Ron, Shona slipped back into the empty flat, whipped out her pen and kneeled down so that she could write something on the underside of the window sill: "Shona was here".

"What you doing?" Dad called out from down below.

"Just going to the loo," Shona called back.

Ron and Dad sat on the seat at the front of Ron's van with Shona sitting between them. The lights in the shops were beaming back at them. She thought of the lovely smell in Zeynep's caff and wondered if there'd be time to slip round to see Nan and get a kebab.

Ron struggled up the stairs with the stuff, muttering and cursing under his breath, Shona doing all she could to help. Dad stood halfway, apologizing, saying that he really would help if he could.

Inside, Shona took it all in. There was one room where they would cook and eat, where they would watch TV and where Dad would sleep. There was a little, tiny room for her. And a shower room for them both.

"One-bedroom flat, they call it, Ron," Dad said.

Ron wasn't up for a chat. He had only come to help because Nan said that he owed it her. He said he didn't. She said he did. She won.

Dad started fishing in his pocket to give Ron something for the work, but Ron waved him away. "She'd kill me if I took anything for this," he said with a grim sort of a laugh.

Shona looked up sharply.

Dad laughed too. "Not really, girl," he said to her. "It's just a way of saying things."

Shona went into her little room and sat on the bed. Very, very slowly she lay down and put her head on the mattress and smelled it as deeply and slowly as she could. Who had been there before?

"Your bed stuff's in that green plastic bag over there," Dad said, and his voice sounded as kind as it ever had. "Hey, come here, girl," he said.

"Mm?" said Shona, not wanting any sort of slushy stuff from Dad just now.

"We'll manage," he said to her and went to ruffle her hair.

She ducked, moving out of his reach. *No one touches my hair. Ever!* she said to herself.

A glance of sadness passed between them. He knew that nowadays she had places in her mind and life that he would never know about, never reach. She knew that too, and it was something that she hugged to herself.

In great families, when an advantageous place cannot be obtained for a young man who is growing up, it is a custom to send him to sea. The board, in imitation of so wise an example, decided to ship off Oliver Twist in some small trading vessel bound to a good unhealthy port. This was the very best thing that could possibly be done with him: the probability being, that the skipper would flog him to death, in a playful mood some day after dinner, or would knock his brains out with an iron bar; both pastimes being, as is pretty generally known, very favourite and common recreations among gentlemen of that class.

Mr Bumble had been sent to make various preliminary inquiries, with the view of finding out some captain or other who wanted a cabin boy without any friends; and was returning to the workhouse to communicate the result of his mission when he encountered Mr Sowerberry, the undertaker, at the gate.

Mr Sowerberry was a tall, gaunt, large-jointed man, attired in a suit of threadbare black, with darned cotton stockings of the same colour, and shoes to match. His features were not naturally intended to wear a smiling aspect, but he was in general rather given to professional lightheartedness. His step was elastic, and his face betokened inward pleasantry, as he advanced to Mr Bumble, and shook him cordially by the hand.

"I have taken the measurements of the two women that died last night, Mr Bumble," said the undertaker.

"You'll make your fortune, Mr Sowerberry," said the beadle, as he thrust his thumb and forefinger into the proffered snuffbox of the undertaker: which was an ingenious little model of a patent coffin.

A 'prentis, who is at present a dead weight; a millstone, as I may say, round the parish throat? Liberal terms, Mr Sowerberry, liberal terms?" As Mr Bumble spoke, he raised his cane to the bill above him, and gave three distinct raps upon the words "five pounds": which were printed thereon in Roman capitals of gigantic size.

"Oh!" replied the undertaker; "why,

you know, Mr Bumble, I pay a good deal towards the poor's rates."

"Hem!" said Mr Bumble. "Well?"

"Well," replied the undertaker, "I was thinking that if I pay so much towards 'em, I've a right to get as much out of 'em as I can, Mr Bumble; and so - I think I'll take the boy myself."

Mr Bumble grasped the undertaker by the arm, and led him into the building. Mr Sowerberry was closeted with the board for five minutes; and it was arranged that Oliver should go to him that evening "upon liking" - a phrase which means, in the case of a parish apprentice, that if the master finds, upon a short trial, that he can get enough work out of a boy without putting too much food into him, he shall have him for a term of years, to do what he likes with.

Little Oliver was taken before "the gentlemen" that evening and informed that he was to go, that night, as general house lad to a coffin maker's; and that if he complained of his situation, or ever came back to the parish again, he would be sent to sea, there to be drowned, or knocked on the head, as the case might be. He showed so little emotion that they by common consent pronounced him a hardened young rascal and ordered Mr Bumble to remove him forthwith.

He heard the news of his destination in perfect silence, and, having had his luggage put into his hand – which was not very difficult to carry, inasmuch as it was all comprised within the limits of a brown paper parcel, about half a foot square by three inches deep – he pulled his cap over his eyes and, once more attaching himself to Mr Bumble's coat cuff, was led away by that dignitary to a new scene of suffering.

The undertaker, who had just put up the shutters of his shop, was making some

"He's very small."

"Why, he is rather small," replied Mr Bumble, looking at Oliver as if it were his fault that he was no bigger. "He is small. There's no denying it. But he'll grow, Mrs Sowerberry, he'll grow."

"Ah! I dare say he will," replied the lady pettishly, "on our food and our drink. I see no saving in parish children, not I; for they always cost more to keep than they're worth. However, men always think they know best. There! Get downstairs, little bag o' bones."

With this, the undertaker's wife opened a side door and pushed Oliver down a steep flight of stairs into a stone cell, damp and dark: forming the anteroom to the coal cellar, and called the "kitchen"; wherein sat a slatternly girl, in shoes down at heel, and blue worsted stockings very much out of repair.

"Here, Charlotte," said Mr Sowerberry,

who had followed Oliver down, "give this boy some of the cold bits that were put by for the dog. He hasn't come home since the morning, so he may go without 'em. I dare say the boy isn't too dainty to eat 'em - are you, boy?"

Oliver, whose eyes had glistened at the mention of meat, and who was trembling with eagerness to devour it, replied in the negative; and a plateful of coarse, broken food was set before him.

"Well," said the undertaker's wife, when Oliver had finished his supper: which she had regarded in silent horror, and with fearful visions of his future appetite: "have you done?"

There being nothing eatable within his reach, Oliver replied in the affirmative.

"Then come with me," said Mrs Sowerberry, taking up a dim and dirty lamp, and leading the way upstairs. "Your bed's under the counter. You don't mind sleeping among the coffins, I suppose? But it doesn't much matter whether you do or don't, for you can't sleep anywhere else. Come; don't keep me here all night!"

Oliver lingered no longer, but meekly followed his new mistress.

Chapter 6

Right up to Thursday night, Shona wondered what a D8 would be like. Whoever she asked either thought that the question was some kind of joke, or they just shrugged. The most she got out of anyone was that you sat there and at some time or another a teacher would ask you some stuff.

She had told Dad that she got a D8, and he took her side in it, saying he would come up to school and tell them that it wasn't her fault that she didn't have a lanyard.

She said it wouldn't make any difference, it was in the system.

"What system?"

"There's this internet thing just for the school. It's called School4U, and they put all the homework up on there but also D8 stuff."

"Blimey, in my day, the teacher just put it up on the board, and I remember this time when the teacher forgot and—"

"—and your mate Jaffo said, 'Oi, sir, you've forgotten to give us homework!' and you lot gave him the beats."

"Did I tell you that one before?"

Shona nodded.

Dad sat thinking for a moment. Even school was different. School4U? "Hang on a minute, girl, we haven't got the internet. How are you getting this Schools4U?"

"School4U, it is. I get it from the ITC room at 3.30 and they just do a printout of anything I need."

"You never shown me that."

"No. I know."

Dad shook his head, like a dog, as if he was trying to get rid of something: a thought, a sense that he wasn't keeping up and never would.

Shona was standing in the mouth of room 3.01 where the D8 was happening. She looked in and it struck her immediately as a place that she didn't want to be, with people she didn't want to be with. The look that came back to her was kind of leery, looking her up and down, like, "what's a little girl like you doing in a place where us lot hang out?" There was no teacher in the room yet, a teacher who might perhaps be some sort of shield against these looks and leers.

She pretended she hadn't noticed and sat herself down apart from these bigger, older kids, winding their legs round chairs, pushing at the tables like they were in the way of important, cool stuff that kids like them would do or could do, given a chance.

Shona waited.

One boy said, "Is your name Sheena?"

She didn't answer.

"Hey," he said a bit louder, "is your name Sheena?"

"No," she said.

"Shona?" he said.

"Yes," she said.

"Kerpow!" he said as if he had hit some kind of target with a dart, or a bullet.

"How did you know her name?" one of his mates asked him.

He just tapped the side of his nose.

"Do you know which teacher's doing this D8?" the first boy asked her.

She just shook her head.

"You could look it up on School4U, couldn't you?"

"It's not me that wants to know, though, is it?" she said.

The other boy clapped. "That's told him," he said.

"Yeah," said the first boy, "but you want to do

me a favour, because I knew your name."

"Look it up yourself," she said.

"I will, then," he said and he took out a phone. He started tapping the keys.

The other boy said, "It won't be on there anyway."

"It will," said the first, "the one who does the D8 is the same as the 'Duty' teacher, isn't it, Shona?"

Shona ignored the question.

"I can't find it on here – I think there's too much stuff on it, and School4U won't upload. Can you try on yours? Pleeeeeeeze?"

"I haven't got a phone."

A hush went round the room. Even people not listening to the conversation went quiet. The sentence "I haven't got a phone" was so odd, so strange, so shocking that it seemed to freeze the room.

The one person who wasn't fazed by it, though, was the boy who knew her name, who had asked the question. He just fished into his pocket, pulled out a second phone and slid it across the table at Shona.

Shona didn't touch it.

"Oh well, don't worry about it," he said.

So Shona slid it back towards him.

"No, no," he said, "have it anyway," and back it went towards her.

She looked at him. Was he kidding? What was going on?

"Have it," he repeated.

The second boy leered and said, "It doesn't work.

It's like one of those toy phones they give babies."

"Sling it back, Shona," said the first boy.

Shona slid it back across the table and it caught the light as it flew.

The boy picked it up and pressed a few keys, and in a second it was playing the trailer of a movie that had only come out last week. While it was still playing, he slid it back once more towards Shona and it went on playing Michael Fassbender dropping out of a plane with only half a parachute.

At that precise moment, Lanyard Man walked into the room in a very straight line. Shona quickly pressed "pause" and sat as still as she could.

"Give!" he said to her. "You know the rules. No mobiles turned on in school time."

"It's not school time, sir," said one of the boys on the other side of the class.

"It is," said Lanyard Man, "another D8 for you next Thursday."

He turned to Shona. "You can have this back at the end of the D8. I've heard about you from Miss—"

Shona interrupted him. "It's not mine," she said. "It's his," she added, pointing at the first boy, who was smiling in a nearly nice sort of a way. Well, certainly not in the leery way the other boy did.

"I gave it to her, though," he said.

"I don't care one way or another," said Lanyard Man, "you can sort it out between you at the end of the D8 ... which" – he looked at his watch – "is starting ... NOW!"

Everyone apart from Shona seemed to know that this meant from this point on you said nothing. If you did, your D8 began again, or it was added on to a new one, next week.

There were about ten students in the room. Sitting in silence.

Lanyard Man wrote some things up on the white board:

Do you know why you're here?

Why do you think you did it?

What are you going to do about not doing the same thing again?

Shona stared at the writing.

Do I know why I'm here?

No, she wrote down mentally on an imaginary piece of paper in front of her. I don't know why Lanyard Man didn't wait to hear why I didn't have a lanyard. Or why it all went weird after that about the maths test. But does he mean that? Or does why am I here mean, why were we born? I don't know why I was born. I don't know why things have turned out the way they have.

Why do I think I did it?

I didn't. I didn't deliberately not have a lanyard and I wasn't deliberately rude to Lanyard Man about whether I needed a lanyard to do a maths test. And I didn't have anything to do with being born but— and then, in an awful flash, that old terrible, shaky thought came to her about Mum, and she stifled it and buried it and pushed it back down to where it came from.

What am I going to do about not doing the same thing again?

I don't know. I don't know if for some reason I might not have my lanyard again. I don't know if I might say something in some kind of a way that someone will say is rude and I'll be here again. Stuff happens to me. Like Mum. I don't make stuff happen.

Her mind drifted on and on; she felt herself floating from the classroom, sitting in grumpy Ron's van... Why did he "owe it to Nan", as he said? And then on to the new place, to Zeynep's caff, to Nan – poor Nan – in the market, to that time at the seaside on the school trip when Shona ran so fast that she was the fastest in the whole school and it felt for a moment like she was so not ordinary, she was special ... and way, way back to a beach and she was crying because she couldn't find her bucket and there was Nan and Mum and another woman who brought her an ice cream... Who was that woman?

Little Shona Walker
Sitting in a saucer
Ride Shona ride
Wipe your weeping eyes ...

...and that was it. Lanyard Man said it was all over. He seemed in a hurry and stuffed the bits of paper and books he had been looking at into his bag. Suddenly, he wasn't a fierce, angry man, sticking to the rules; he was a small, very busy, very harassed man who still had the scab on his face from a shaving accident, who had to be somewhere right away, and was already late.

He put the mobile down on Shona's table and said to everyone, "I don't like doing this thing any more than you do. If, next time, you think you're going to do something pointless, useless, rude or unnecessary, spare us all the tedium of having to do a D8. Just think, in a few years' time, you're going to be like me, trying to make a living. Get it right, guys. Get it wrong now and you could end up like my brother."

Shona had no idea who Lanyard Man's brother was, but it seemed as if all the older ones did, and they responded by either nodding or grunting in some kind of knowing way.

At that, the man rushed out of the room, trying

(but not succeeding) to smooth down a spiky bit of hair at the back of his head.

The boy who had tried to give Shona the mobile didn't pick it up. He was halfway out of the room when he turned to her and said, "If you want a phone line on it, so you don't have to depend on Wi-Fi, I can do that for you," he said. "I'll be at Zeynep's – you know, the Kettle Caff – tomorrow night. Around seven."

And he walked out.

Shona was on her own in the room. She hadn't streamed out with the rest. It was just her and the phone, glinting slightly under the lights.

A phone! Internet, apps, YouTube, Snapchat... She almost ached with the longing to have it all for the first time in her life. Should she? Just pick it up. And, yes, she could just go down to Zeynep's tomorrow and if he was there, he would sort it.

No, she shouldn't. She didn't know the boy. What would Dad say? Who knows what Dad would say? He was sinking more and more into his armchair. And he doesn't seem to know anything. No, the best person to ask was herself.

Yes, I'll ask myself: what do you say, Shona?

Well, Shona, I say, pick it up, and see him at Zeynep's tomorrow.

Shona walked over to the phone, picked it up and walked out the room.

Sorted.

CLASS X10 READING COMPREHENSION

"I beg your pardon, sir," said Oliver at length: seeing that no other visitor made his appearance; "did you knock?"

"I kicked," replied the charity-boy.

"Did you want a coffin, sir?" inquired Oliver, innocently.

At this, the charity-boy looked monstrous fierce; and said that Oliver would want one before long, if he cut jokes with his superiors in that way.

"Yer don't know who I am, I suppose, Work'us?" said the charity-boy.

"No, sir," answered Oliver.

"I'm Mister Noah Claypole," said the charity-boy, "and you're under me. Take down the shutters, yer idle young ruffian!" With this, Mr Claypole administered a kick to Oliver, and entered the shop with a dignified air, which did him great credit.

It is difficult for a large-headed, small-eyed youth to look dignified under any circumstances; but it is more especially so, when added to these are a red nose and yellow breeches.

Oliver, having taken down the shutters, and broken a pane of glass in his effort to stagger away beneath the weight of the first one to a small court at the side of the house in which they were kept during the day, was graciously assisted by Noah: who having consoled him with the assurance that "he'd catch it," condescended to help him.

Mr Sowerberry came down soon after. Shortly afterwards, Mrs Sowerberry appeared. Oliver having "caught it," in fulfilment of Noah's prediction, followed that young gentleman down the stairs to breakfast.

"Come near the fire, Noah," said Charlotte. "I saved a nice little bit of bacon for you from master's breakfast. Oliver, shut that door at Mister Noah's back, and take them bits that I've put out on the cover of the bread-pan. There's your tea; take it away to that box, and drink it there, and make haste, for they'll want you to mind the shop. D'ye hear?"

"D'ye hear, Work'us?" said Noah Claypole.

"Lor, Noah!" said Charlotte, "what a rum creature you are! Why don't you let the boy alone?"

"Let him alone!" said Noah. "Why, everybody lets him alone enough. Neither his father nor his mother will ever interfere with him. All his relations let him have his own way pretty well. Eh, Charlotte? He! he! he!"

"Oh, you queer soul!" said Charlotte, bursting into a hearty laugh; after which they both looked scornfully at poor Oliver Twist, as he sat shivering on the box in the coldest corner of the room, and ate the stale pieces which had been specially reserved for him.

Noah was a charity-boy, but not a workhouse orphan. No chance-child was he, for he could trace his genealogy all the way back to his parents, who lived hard by; his mother being a washerwoman, and his father a drunken soldier, discharged with a wooden leg, and a daily pension of twopence-halfpenny and an unstateable fraction. The shop boys in the neighbourhood had long been in the habit of calling Noah insulting names like "leathers", "charity", and the like in the public streets; and Noah had taken them without reply. But, now that fortune had cast in his way a nameless orphan, at whom even the meanest could point the finger of scorn, he took it out on him with interest. This shows us what a beautiful thing human nature may be made to be; and how impartially the same loveable qualities are developed in the finest lord and the dirtiest charity-boy.

Chapter 7

Shona was looking down at her mobile. Miss Cavani was in full flow. She turned it over. And back. And then over again. She was so looking forward to getting the connection.

In fact, she was looking forward to it so much, she didn't notice Miss Cavani creeping over to see what she was doing. Shona slowly became aware that just as Miss Cavani was saying: "...and the Victorians kept the idea of death very much to the forefront, much more than..." that her teacher was now right beside her, watching her turning the mobile over and over in her hand like it was a bit of treasure.

And Miss Cavani did that thing where teachers merge what they're saying about their subject with what's going on in the room: "... us with our obsession with mobile phones, Snapchat, Facebook and the rest."

The class laughed. Miss Cavani stopped talking.

Shona blushed and dropped the mobile into her bag. At least it hadn't been switched on. She might just avoid getting a D8 then.

"If your husband died, Shona, what would you wear?"

It seemed such a bewildering thing to say. She didn't have a husband! What sort of joke was this?

Crayton had his hand up. Miss Cavani nodded.

"Widow's weeds, Miss."

"Excellent, yes. The black shawl, long black dress, the black veil they called 'widow's weeds'. What with people dying young – no modern medicines, remember, and wars – this meant that everywhere you went, you would see this reminder of death. Nowadays, walking down a street, say, you wouldn't know if someone had lost their wife or husband."

Shona would never know why at that very moment something – what was it? A slight noise, the sound of a movement? – made her look round behind her.

Rory was looking across to Sunil – it would be Rory, wouldn't it, so often himself on the end of jeers and sneers – and with an exaggerated hand mime was pointing at Shona while at the same time doing a death line across his neck. The others in the class wondered, what did Rory mean? That he reckoned Shona was in serious trouble with Miss Cavani and was "dead"? Or was he picking up on Miss Cavani saying that Shona's "husband" was dead?

Shona was in no doubt what it meant. For her, it meant that Rory had discovered that Shona's mum was dead and he was looking to get a laugh for pointing it out to the whole class. And the moment she saw it, that fearful, night-time terror got hold of her.

She turned and rose out of her seat in one move and jumped at Rory. One hand reached his throat and the other his face. The one that reached his throat clutched and scratched at it, and the one that reached his face started to hammer at the first part of Rory's face it reached: the side of his nose.

To say Rory wasn't ready for it would be an understatement. He had no inkling, not one jot of a thought that such a thing was going to happen.

So, for a full four seconds, Shona's hands did the damage they were meant to do, by which time Miss Cavani from one side, Désol'é from the other, had grabbed Shona and pulled her away from Rory's face and neck.

The class could hear Rory making sobbing sounds while out of Shona's mouth came a rasping, gasping sound.

Once Miss Cavani had got everyone back in their seats, she had to decide very quickly whether to press on as if nothing had happened or to stop and have a "Cavani Talk". In a split second, she decided that it would be the "nothing happened" routine. She knew – and she reckoned that Shona knew she knew – that there was stuff going on here that just couldn't be talked about in the open.

Everyone in the room, Shona especially, was waiting for those words: "D8" ... or even "D2" ... or even "exclusion". But they didn't come. For some reason, there was going to be a deviation from the usual, an unexpected route round the rock.

Instead, Miss Cavani breathed in with all the

professional skill of an actor, flicked over the pages of her copy of *Oliver Twist* and said, "Oliver Twist, because he looked so miserable, was promoted by the undertaker, Mr Sowerberry, to be a mourner at funerals." She began to read:

CLASS X10 READING COMPREHENSION

... for many months Oliver continued meekly to submit to the domination and ill-treatment of Noah Claypole: who used him far worse than before, now that Noah's jealousy was roused by seeing the new boy promoted to the black stick and hatband, while he, the old one, remained stationary in the muffin cap and leathers. Charlotte treated him ill, because Noah did; and Mrs Sowerberry was his decided enemy, because Mr Sowerberry was disposed to be his friend; so, between these three on one side, and a glut of funerals on the other, Oliver was not altogether as comfortable as a hungry pig shut up, by mistake, in the grain department of a brewery.

One day, Oliver and Noah had descended into the kitchen at the usual dinner hour, to banquet upon a small joint of mutton - a pound and a half of the worst end of the neck - when, Charlotte being called out of the way, there ensued a brief interval of time which Noah Claypole, being hungry and vicious, considered he could not possibly devote to a worthier purpose than aggravating young Oliver Twist.

Noah put his feet on the tablecloth; and pulled Oliver's hair; and twitched his ears; and expressed his opinion that he was a "sneak"; and furthermore announced his intention of coming to see him hanged, whenever that desirable event should take place; and entered upon various topics of petty annoyance, like a malicious and ill-conditioned charity-boy as he was. But, making Oliver cry, Noah attempted to be more facetious still; and in his attempt, did what many sometimes do to this day, when they want to be funny. He got rather personal.

"Work'us," said Noah, "how's your mother?"

"She's dead," replied Oliver; "don't you say anything about her to me!"

Oliver's colour rose as he said this; he breathed quickly; and there was a curious working of the mouth and nostrils, which Mr Claypole thought must be the immediate precursor of a violent fit of crying. Under this impression he returned to the charge.

"What did she die of, Work'us?" said Noah.

"Of a broken heart, some of our old nurses told me," replied Oliver: more as if he were talking to himself, than answering Noah. "I think I know what it must be to die of that!"

"Tol de rol lol lol, right fol lairy, Work'us," said Noah, as a tear rolled down Oliver's cheek. "What's set you a-snivelling now?"

"Not you," replied Oliver, sharply. "There; that's enough. Don't say anything more to me about her; you'd better not!"

"Better not!" exclaimed Noah. "Well! Better not! Work'us, don't be impudent. Your mother, too! She was a nice 'un she was. Oh, Lor!" And here, Noah nodded his head expressively; and curled up as much of his small red nose as muscular action could collect together, for the occasion.

"Yer know, Work'us," continued Noah, emboldened by Oliver's silence, and speaking in a jeering tone of affected pity: of all tones the most annoying: "Yer know, Work'us, it can't be helped now; and of course yer couldn't help it then; and I am very sorry for it; and I'm sure we all are, and pity yer very much. But yer must know, Work'us, yer mother was a regular right-down bad 'un."

"What did you say?" inquired Oliver, looking up very quickly.

"A regular right-down bad 'un, Work'us," replied Noah, coolly. "And it's a great deal better, Work'us, that she died when she did, or else she'd have been hard labouring in Bridewell, or transported, or hung; which is more likely than either, isn't it?"

Crimson with fury, Oliver started up; overthrew the chair and table; seized Noah by the throat; shook him, in the violence of his rage, till his teeth chattered in his head; and collecting his whole force into one heavy blow, felled him to the ground.

A minute ago, the boy had looked the quiet child, mild, dejected creature that harsh treatment had made him. But his spirit was roused at last; the cruel insult to his dead mother had set his blood on fire. His breast heaved; his attitude was erect; his eyes bright and vivid; his whole person changed, as he stood glaring over the cowardly tormentor who now lay crouching at his feet; and defied him with an energy

he had never known before.

"He'll murder me!" blubbered Noah. "Charlotte! Missis! Here's the new boy a murdering of me! Help! help! Oliver's gone mad! Char-lotte!"

Noah's shouts were responded to by a loud scream from Charlotte, and a louder one from Mrs Sowerberry; the former of whom rushed into the kitchen by a side door, while the latter paused on the staircase till she was quite certain that it was consistent with the preservation of human life to come further down.

"Oh, you little wretch!" screamed Charlotte: seizing Oliver with her utmost force, which was about equal to that of a moderately strong man in particularly good training. "Oh, you little un-grate-ful, mur-de-rous, hor-rid villain!" And between every syllable, Charlotte gave Oliver a blow with all her might: accompanying it with a scream.

Charlotte's fist was by no means a light one; but, lest it should not be effective in calming Oliver's wrath, Mrs Sowerberry plunged into the kitchen, and assisted to hold him with one hand, while she scratched his face with the other. In this favourable position of affairs, Noah rose from the ground, and pommelled him behind.

This was rather too violent an exercise to last long. When they were all wearied out, and could tear and beat no longer, they dragged Oliver, struggling and shouting, but not daunted, into the dust-cellar, and there locked him up. This being done, Mrs Sowerberry sunk into a chair, and burst into tears.

"Bless her, she's going off!" said Charlotte. "A glass of water, Noah, dear. Make haste!"

"Oh! Charlotte," said Mrs Sowerberry: speaking as well as she could, through a deficiency of breath, and a sufficiency of cold water, which Noah had poured over her head and shoulders. "Oh! Charlotte, what a mercy we have not all been murdered in our beds!"

"Ah! mercy indeed, ma'am," was the reply. "I only hope this'll teach master not to have any more of these dreadful creatures, that are born to be murderers and robbers from their very cradle. Poor Noah! He was all but killed, ma'am, when I come in."

"Poor fellow!" said Mrs Sowerberry: looking piteously on the charity-boy.

Noah, whose top waistcoat button might have been somewhere on a level with the crown of Oliver's head, rubbed his eyes with the inside of his wrists while this commiseration was bestowed upon him, and performed some affecting tears and sniffs.

"What's to be done!" exclaimed Mrs Sowerberry. "Your master's not at home; there's not a man in the house, and he'll kick that door down in ten minutes." Oliver's vigorous plunges against the bit of timber in question rendered this highly probable.

"Dear, dear! I don't know, ma'am," said Charlotte, "unless we send for the police officers."

"Or the millingtary," suggested Mr Claypole.

Chapter 8

The lesson was over and Shona sat opposite Miss Cavani in the place that Miss Cavani laughingly called her "suite". In truth it was a cupboard at the edge of the drama studio.

And Miss Cavani was not really in a laughing mood; she was being "firm". She was sitting as upright as the pillar by the school gates and repeating the word "no".

"No, no, no, no, no!"

This was to try to impress on Shona that she

had got it completely wrong about Rory, that she, Miss Cavani, had had a long talk with Rory and was quite certain that Rory didn't mean anything whatsoever to do with Shona's mother for the very simple reason that it was quite clear to Miss Cavani that Rory *didn't know that Shona's mother had died*. His gestures were, it seems, said Miss Cavani, something to do with how Shona was in trouble or going to get in trouble or some silly stuff that was in Rory's head.

"Sometimes," said Miss Cavani, doing her best not to sound too contemptuous, "boys can't – how shall I put it – express their feelings of affection or admiration for girls – and, er ... so, do the opposite."

Shona didn't know how to respond to all this. As far as she was concerned, Rory was laughing at her and at the fact that she had no mum and this was bad, totally bad, and there was no way back from that. Even so, the hard truth of what Miss Cavani was saying was, bit by bit, filtering through to her un-angry, un-raging self. Perhaps Rory was just being an idiot. Is that it? And she had strangled him for that? OK, not strangled, but damaged.

"You know I could have given you a D8 or a D2, Shona," Miss Cavani said. "If I had really wanted to, I could have had you excluded. But look here; I think it's more important we go forward together on this. I don't want to lose you. If I bring the full weight of the system down on top of your head, I can well imagine that you'll go off the rails, start hanging out with – well, I won't say – but as I'm sure you know there are some types in the school who it'll be very much in your interest to steer very clear of. You do understand that, don't you?"

Shona only half-heard this. Speeches from teachers were hard to hear. Well, you could hear them, but you couldn't always "get" them. What did "steer clear of" actually mean? Where do you steer to? Who's doing the steering? And what were the "rails"? Where are the "rails"?

"Now you're late," said Miss Cavani, cutting into Shona's daydreaming. "You'd better let your dad know where you are. Have you got a phone?"

"Yeah," said Shona, pulling it out, "but it doesn't work."

"Doesn't work?" said Miss Cavani, her antennae bristling. She knew about phones that didn't work all right. Oh yes, she knew about phones passing hands, phones that mysteriously appeared and disappeared even if she wasn't a hundred per cent sure where they came from.

She feigned ignorance. "Oh dear," she said, "will you take it to the shop to get it sorted?"

"No," said Shona, unaware that she was walking into the great big hole that Miss Cavani had carefully dug one second before, "there's a … er … a … I'm… I've…" Her voice petered out as she realized for herself that there was something odd about a boy higher up the school giving out a phone and then saying that he could get it to work.

"Oh, you know someone," Miss Cavani said with as little suspicion in her voice as she could conjure up. "I've heard there are one or two boys in the upper school who are good at phones."

"Yes," said Shona.

"Yes," said Miss Cavani.

But that was it. Miss Cavani could see that there wasn't going to be any more coming from Shona on this.

And Shona knew that there was something going on in the room that made her uneasy. She liked Miss Cavani. She liked her a lot, but not so much that she was going to risk not having YouTube, Snapchat and the rest at her fingertips.

"For the next two weeks, Shona, at the end of the day, I want you to come and see me in my suite here, and you're going to tell me about all the good things that have happened in the previous 24 hours and – if there are any – any bad. Now that's going to be better than a D8 or a D2, isn't it?"

Shona nodded.

"How are you getting on with the *Oliver* book?"

"OK," Shona said.

"Right, a little tip for you here so that you can jump on ahead: Oliver is badly beaten by Mr Sowerberry, so Oliver runs away. We've all had dreams of doing that one day, haven't we, eh?" Miss Cavani laughed.

Shona looked puzzled. Miss Cavani had dreamed of running away? She, Shona, definitely had, but Miss Cavani? Didn't she have it all just right? Nice job, nice clothes, nice looks.

"So Oliver gets himself to London, he's starving, freezing cold and, well, he's nearly dead. He's lying by the side of the road ... as I say, nearly dead. There," said Miss Cavani, handing Shona the next printout of the book, "carry on from there."

CLASS X10 READING COMPREHENSION

"Hullo, my covey! What's the row?"

The boy who addressed this inquiry was about his own age, but one of the queerest-looking boys that Oliver had ever seen. He was a snub-nosed, flat-browed, common-faced boy; and as dirty a juvenile as one would wish to see; but he had about him all the airs and manners of a man. He was short for his age: with rather bow-legs, and little, sharp, ugly eyes. His hat was stuck on the top of his head so lightly that it threatened to fall off every moment - and would have done so, very often, if the wearer had not had a knack of every now and then giving his head a sudden twitch, which brought it back to its old place again. He wore a man's coat, which reached nearly to his heels. He had turned the cuffs back, halfway up his arm, to get his hands out of the sleeves: apparently with the ultimate view of thrusting them into the pockets of his corduroy trousers; for there he kept them. He was, altogether, as roystering and swaggering a young gentleman as ever stood four feet six, or something less, in half-boots.

"Hullo, my covey! What's the row?" said this strange young gentleman to Oliver.

"I am very hungry and tired," replied Oliver: the tears standing in his eyes as he spoke.

"I have walked a long way. I have been walking these seven days."

"Walking for sivin days!" said the young gentleman. "Oh, I see. Beak's order, eh? But," he added, noticing Oliver's look of surprise, "I suppose you don't know what a beak is, my flash com-pan-i-on."

Oliver mildly replied that he had always heard a bird's mouth described by the term in question.

"My eyes, how green!" exclaimed the young gentleman. "Why, a beak's a madgst'rate; and when you walk by a beak's order, it's not straight forerd, but always agoing up, and niver a coming down agin. Was you never on the mill?"

"What mill?" inquired Oliver.

"What mill! Why, the mill – the mill as takes up so little room that it'll work inside a Stone Jug; and always goes better when the wind's low with people, than when it's high; acos then they can't get workmen.

But come," said the young gentleman, "you want grub, and you shall have it. I'm at low-water mark myself - only one bob and a magpie; but, as far as it goes, I'll fork out and stump. Up with you on your pins. There! Now then!"

Assisting Oliver to rise, the young gentleman took him to an adjacent shop, where he purchased a sufficiency of ready-dressed ham and a half-quartern loaf. Taking the bread under his arm, the young gentleman turned into a small public house, and led the way to a taproom in the rear of the premises. Here, a pot of beer was brought in, by direction of the mysterious youth; and Oliver, falling to, at his new friend's bidding, ate a long and hearty meal, during the progress of which the strange boy eyed him from time to time with great attention.

"Going to London?" said the strange boy, when Oliver had at length concluded.

"Yes."

"Got any lodgings?"

"No."

"Money?"

"No."

The strange boy whistled; and put his arms into his pockets, as far as the big coat sleeves would let them go.

"Do you live in London?" inquired Oliver.

"Yes. I do, when I'm at home," replied the boy. "I suppose you want some place to sleep in tonight, don't you?"

"I do, indeed," answered Oliver. "I have not slept under a roof since I left the country."

"Don't fret your eyelids on that score," said the young gentleman. "I've got to be in London tonight; and I know a 'spectable old gentleman as lives there, wot'll give you lodgings for nothink, and never ask for the change - that is, if any genelman he knows interduces you. And don't he know me? Oh, no! Not in the least! By no means. Certainly not!"

The young gentleman smiled, as if to indicate that he was being playfully ironical; and finished the beer as he did so.

Chapter 9

*I*t was Thursday. Shona sat in the caff. She'd asked Zeynep if she could sit in for a while with a glass of water; she was meeting someone. Again, there was that gorgeous smell of kebabs and chips and pitta bread in her nostrils. She felt the tug of her stomach and watched longingly as Mevlut laid the kebab sticks over the glowing charcoal.

She put the phone on the table in front of her and conjured up for herself a picture of her tapping away, sharing pics, listening to whatever she wanted to. She checked to see if there was any Wi-Fi nearby. No. Nothing. She spun the phone round on itself. She slid it across the table and back and sipped the water. Everyone, but everyone, had a phone. Except her.

"Hey!"

It was the boy. He smiled. Beyond him, Shona caught a glimpse of Zeynep. She was staring at the boy and her. There was shock in that look.

Oh no, Shona thought, Zeynep thinks it's a date! Oh no, it's nothing like that. He's, like, fifteen or sixteen... This meeting's not a date – sure he looks nice – but no, no, no, this is all about the phone. Isn't it?

The boy sat down. He nodded at the glass of water. "You want something?"

"One of those frothy coffees?" Shona said cautiously. *Look at me,* she thought, *I'm giving coffee a try.*

"Sure."

He got up, swung himself over to Zeynep and

swung back. He picked up the phone, turned it over, pressed bits of it and put it down. "What it is, yeah... I mean, what it is, yeah, is that I can't sort this right now. I mean, I've got to see someone so it can ... like, go through."

Shona looked at him. Was he lying?

"The thing is, it's, like, the guy I'm seeing about this? You won't understand, but I owe him."

That "owing" thing again. Everyone round here talks about "owing him" or "owing her". How did it work?

"I've got to do him, like, a favour, and I'm thinking ... like, you could see your way to helping me here ... and then, like, I'm tight with him, and you get your phone and we're all cool, yeah?"

As he spoke, it was as if the light of the phone screen came and went. One moment, it was in her hand and she was texting and watching stuff on YouTube and the next it was just as it was right now: dark, flat and still.

I want that phone, I want that phone, she heard herself saying in her head and her fingers played across the smoothness of the screen.

The boy looked at his watch and stood up. Shona watched him as he went from being one moment his usual lolling-on-a-chair self, to the next being Busy Guy in all of a hurry. "So, it's like this, yeah? I have to do fetch-and-carry for this guy who – like, you won't believe how lazy he is, yeah – I've got to pick up some stuff from LQ Sports for him, but…" He looked at his watch again, as if it was already ages and ages since the last time he looked at it, "But, I've got some other, like, stuff to do, so I'm asking you if you can get it to him for me, and then, I can sort the phone thing."

Shona took a sip of the coffee; she didn't know whether she liked it or not. She nodded.

"What it is, yeah," he said, "is there's Gazz, he's picking up this stuff from LQ, and he'll, like, give you the bag, and all you got to do is nip round the corner in that side road, Glenarm Close, and another mate of mine, he'll be standing next to a white Bimmer. You give it to him, and that's it. And at the end of it you get your phone."

It seemed to make sense. Kind of. So all she had to do was take a bag from someone she had never met and give it to someone else she had never met.

The boy was on to it. "You know Gazz. He's the one who was with me in the D8."

She nodded. She hoped outside she looked cool and OK with it, while inside it was beginning to make her jumpy.

"You don't know Al, but you'll see the white Bimmer and he'll be right next to it. In Glenarm ... and I'll sort your phone."

"When?" Shona asked.

"That's what I mean," the boy said, looking at his watch again, "*now*, you hear what I'm saying?" He gestured to her to get up and get moving but before she left, he took the phone back off her.

"Have I got time to say hello to my nan? She's just over there, on the odds-and-ends stall."

The boy looked from Shona to outside, in the direction of Nan's stall, and back. "Yeah. No. Look, no. I'm, like, really pressed, OK. Let's do this thing now. Just go into LQ and go to the ladies' section. Oh yeah, once he's given it to you, keep moving, yeah? Like, everyone's pressed, eh? Pressure!" And he said "pressure" as if it was two words: "presh" and "ure" with a big hit on the "ure" bit. He was almost pushing her out the door as he hopped from one foot to the other.

Shona kept her head down. *Brand new trainers,* she thought, looking down at his feet.

She headed across the road and down the street in the opposite direction from Nan's stall. She'd drop by to see her in a minute.

In LQ, it was the usual crush, with people holding up trackie bottoms against each other, boys staring at football boots like they were jewels, old guys in sports outfits hoping it made them look young, skinny women in tight, stretched, pink-and-purple running gear, babies crying, overweight security guys strolling between the puffer jackets. She walked over to the ladies' department and waited, looking at the video of someone beautiful running, and there, suddenly, was Gazz. Just like the boy had said – *Funny*, a thought went through her mind: *how come I know Gazz's name but not the boy's name?* – and in that instant, he handed her a bag.

Keep moving – she remembered what the boy said and she slipped out the shop. If everyone is under so much pressure (presh – URE!) then, *yeah, I can do people a favour … and I get my phone … and if I'm any good at it, maybe I can do a bit of fetch and carry, and get paid for it … maybe…* and by now she was in Glenarm Close, and sure enough, there was a white Bimmer and a boy was standing next to it, and she handed him the bag.

"Yeah, cool," he said, and he slipped away almost before she had looked at him.

She turned round, feeling slightly odd. It had all happened so quick and so easy and then she remembered that she hadn't made a deal with him for when he'd give her back the phone, all connected up. Hey, that felt wrong… What if he wasn't going to, and it was all some kind of trick? But for what?

She picked her way through the crowd in the market up to Nan's stall. Nan was dealing with a customer, so didn't say hi at first.

When it was clear, she said, without looking at Shona, "Been busy, have you?"

"Yes," Shona said.

"Zeynep tells me you're meeting up with boys now."

"Oh, yes, but no, it's not like that, Nan. No, it's this boy from my school who's sorting me out a phone."

"I know," said Nan.

A punter came and bought a pack of batteries. Nan dealt with it.

"Look, love," said Nan, "you be careful."

"I know," said Shona, feeling ratty that Nan was wagging her finger at her, thinking that it was about dating-stuff again.

"I mean, we all have to take risks," Nan said, "just to get by, but..." Her voice faded into the jostle and cries of the market.

"How you feeling, Nan?"

"Oh, don't mind me. We all have to go sometime."

"Don't talk like that. You'll be all right."

Nan smiled the smile of someone who had settled in and was ready for whatever would happen.

She whistled "Que Sera, Sera. Whatever will be, will be..."

That was Nan's favourite whistle: she'd say something big that had happened. She'd shrug. And then whistle "Que Sera, Sera". Like whenever she mentioned Lorraine. "Oh yes," she'd say, "took herself off to New York. We're not good enough for her. Still, there you go…" And that would be the signal to do the whistle. It was Nan's way of saying "The End" of the chat.

"I've got to get back now," Shona said. "I promised I'd get in some stuff for Dad." She gave Nan a kiss.

"How is it you know Tino?" asked Nan quietly.

Oh, so it wasn't the end of the chat. Shona realized she had said something important enough for Nan to want it to go on.

"Who's Tino?" said Shona.

"The boy you were with, in Zeynep's."

Shona was just about to mention the D8 but then— "How do you know his name's Tino?" she asked.

Nan stopped still. It was like she had been caught in a photo. "Tino," she said as if that explained something, "you know, the one Zeynep said you were with…"

"Right, yeah," Shona said.

Nan helped a few more customers, Shona watched Nan's fingers tickling the coins in her bowl as she handed out change.

"I'm off now, Nan," and went to give Nan a hug, but Nan turned herself sideways to avoid being hugged head on.

"Sorry," Shona said, not wanting to give Nan even the slightest twinge, let alone pain of any kind.

"You take care, angel," Nan said, kissing her cheek. Shona strolled off towards the flat – really it was just that room, where Dad would be sitting on the beat-up sofa. She had the feeling there was something sad about the way they had said goodbye … about the way Nan had said "we all have to go sometime".

Huh! That's no way to talk, she thought to herself as she was nearly bowled over the rush of people coming out of the train station.

A rolled-up bit of paper with a blob of old chewing gum inside it hit the side of Shona's head. She ignored it.

Miss Cavani walked in and the room slipped into quiet. As she breathed in to begin the lesson, Rasheda put her hand up. It seemed urgent.

"I've read ahead, Miss, and it's racist. I don't think we should be reading this stuff. You know, all that British Values, and stuff that we're doing in PCHE, and we all said how we've all got to be tolerant, and we're reading this."

As she said "this", she threw down a copy of the whole book that she had got from the library.

"Anyone else read ahead?" Miss Cavani looked round the room.

It seemed not.

"Right," she went on. "What I'm going to propose is that we read on and then talk about it. Otherwise it's just me and Rasheda having a discussion about something that no one else has looked at."

"No, but what I'm saying, Miss, is I don't think we should."

"Why not?"

"Because it makes people believe bad stuff."

"Is that what happened to you? Did you read it and then suddenly start to believe bad stuff?"

"No, but I'm…" Rasheda stopped.

Miss Cavani waited.

"Well, let's read it and talk about it in a minute," Miss Cavani said, smoothing down the hair on both sides of her head.

Now everyone's attention was wound up. Who was going to be racist about who? Was Oliver going to be racist about another boy? Was there some kind of trick where in fact it turned out that Oliver was mixed race and these other kids were teasing him, or what?

Miss Cavani, said, "So, where were we? Ah, yes. Remember, the strange boy who met Oliver and took him to the pub? This boy's name was Jack Dawkins, also known as the Artful Dodger, whom you may have heard of before…"

The boy threw open the door of a back room, and drew Oliver in after him.

The walls and ceiling of the room were perfectly black with age and dirt. There was a deal table before the fire: upon which were a candle, stuck in a ginger-beer bottle, two or three pewter pots, a loaf and butter, and a plate. In a frying pan, which was on the fire, and which was secured to the mantelshelf by a string, some sausages were cooking; and standing over them, with a toasting fork in his hand, was a very old shrivelled Jew, whose villainous-looking and repulsive face was obscured by a quantity of matted red hair. He was dressed in a greasy flannel gown, with his throat bare; and seemed to be dividing his attention between the frying pan and the clothes horse, over which a great number of silk handkerchiefs were hanging. Several rough beds made of old sacks were huddled side by side on the floor. Seated round the table were four or five boys, none older than the Dodger, smoking long clay pipes, and drinking spirits with the air of middle-aged men. These all crowded about their

associate as he whispered a few words to the Jew; and then turned round and grinned at Oliver. So did the Jew himself, toasting fork in hand.

"This is him, Fagin," said Jack Dawkins, "my friend, Oliver Twist."

The Jew grinned and, making a low bow to Oliver, took him by the hand, and said he hoped he should have the honour of his intimate acquaintance. Upon this, the young gentleman with the pipes came round him, and shook both his hands very hard - especially the one in which he held his little bundle. One young gentleman was very anxious to hang up his cap for him; and another was so obliging as to put his hands in his pockets, in order that, as he was very tired, he might not have the trouble of emptying them, himself, when he went to bed. These civilities would probably be extended much farther, but for a liberal exercise of the Jew's toasting fork on the heads and shoulders of the affectionate youths who offered them.

"We are very glad to see you, Oliver, very," said the Jew. "Dodger, take off the sausages; and draw a tub near the fire for Oliver. Ah, you're a-staring at the pocket handkerchiefs, eh, my dear! There are a good many of 'em, ain't there? We've just looked 'em out, ready for the wash; that's all, Oliver; that's all. Ha! ha! ha!"

The latter part of this speech was hailed by a boisterous shout from all the hopeful pupils of the merry old gentleman. In the midst of which they went to supper.

Oliver ate his share, and the Jew then mixed him a glass of hot gin and water, telling him he must drink it off directly, because another gentleman wanted the glass. Oliver did as he was desired. Immediately afterwards he felt himself gently lifted onto one of the sacks; and then he sunk into a deep sleep.

"The thing is," Rasheda said, "you can't say these things. It's like hate crime."

"It is so not a hate crime," Rory dived in. "Hate crime is like if I say to you…" he stopped.

"Say to me what?" said Rasheda looking at him straight between the eyes.

Shona took it in and could see why he had stopped.

Harry helped: "Hate crime is where you try to get people to attack other people because, say, they're disabled."

They all knew Harry might know what he was talking about, because his sister was disabled.

Désol'é said, "My mum says that my granddad was in Washington when Martin Luther King did that 'I have a dream' speech."

"Yeah, right," said Crayton, who didn't believe anything Désol'é said.

She chipped back at him: "Your granddad lives in a skip."

Shona laughed at Désol'é's line and then stopped herself.

Miss Cavani clapped her hands.

Sunil put his hand up.

"Yes?" said Miss Cavani, knowing that it was a risk to allow Sunil to speak in a discussion about something as sensitive as this.

Sunil looked round and said, "There's a crazy old guy in our flats who talks to himself, and sometimes when someone goes by he shouts, 'Wolla wolla Jew boy'. He doesn't know what he's saying, though. He sings all sorts of stuff."

"That's what I'm saying," Rasheda shouted. "This book just stirs all that up, the way it keeps going on about 'the Jew' and how repulsive he is. Why are we doing this book anyway?"

"Ah, well," said Miss Cavani, "that's a long story."

"You mean the book is," said Sunil.

Yes, he could be relied on for a gag, Miss Cavani thought. "Right, X10, the reason why we end up doing one book rather than another in school is because that's what the government want us to do. But..." Miss Cavani held her hand up before a wave of comments reached her. "We can choose some other old English books that were written before 1900, but a good many people think that there is something very special about this one."

Rasheda wasn't letting go. "But it's racist, Miss, you know it is."

Impressive, Shona thought, the way she says things so in-your-face, but with all the right words to back it up.

"What if you were a Jew?" Serena said, more to herself than to anyone in particular. "You'd feel awful reading this."

Harry coughed and started to speak. "I'm … well, not me … and not actually my Mum or Dad, but, like, further back, on my Dad's side … er … I think it's my great-grandfather, he was Jewish."

Is he saying that he is a Jew, or he is not a Jew? Shona asked herself.

"Your parents should write a letter to say that they don't think it's right that we're reading this stuff," Rasheda said to Harry.

A picture came into Miss Cavani's mind of Rasheda in twenty years' time, standing with one hand on her hip in a courtroom, saying, "And do you, do you, ladies and gentlemen of the jury, seriously think that this ... this ... *excuse* for a book, full of volleys of antisemitic abuse, is suitable material for young school students?"

"Why don't we write to Charles Dickens?" said Sunil.

It woke Miss Cavani from her daydream. Was this another one of Sunil's jokes, or did he really think Charles Dickens was still alive?

"Yeah," said Crayton, "I'll text him."

"One of the reasons we're reading this book is to learn how people thought about this sort of thing a hundred and fifty years years ago," Miss Cavani said.

"Some people still think like that," Rasheda said, not letting go.

"That is so right," Désol'é said.

"Letters!" Miss Cavani suddenly cried. "You

know, X10, there are times when I am proud to know you. Yes! We'll all write to Charles Dickens. It doesn't matter he's not alive to read them; we can imagine it. Write in your letter what you really think about the way he's written about Fagin."

"It's a deal," Rasheda said.

Amazing girl, thought Miss Cavani.

Chapter 10

"Get some chips, then," Dad said, rummaging deep in his pocket for some cash.

They'd had chips the night before. And the night before that. Sometimes he stood at the cooker, poking a bit of bacon round the pan, but now he seemed like he didn't have the energy to do that. This move had taken the last bit of stuffing out of him. *Later, I'll put the picture of Mum up somewhere near my bed,* Shona thought, night terrors or not.

"I don't think Nan's all right," Shona said.

"I know. How many times have you told me that?"

"Hmm," Shona grunted.

"She does go on a bit, you know," he said. "When I first met your mother, Nan was 'half-dead', she told me."

"No, no, I think she's really not all right," Shona said, annoyed that he could turn it round like it was Nan making it up.

"If you want to believe her, girl, you believe her."

Shona tutted loudly as her eyes went up into her head and she walked out, banging the door.

As she waited in line at the chip shop, Tino and Gazz swung round the corner. Gazz saw her, nudged Tino, and they came up to her.

"Been looking for you, to give you your phone. I've sorted it," Tino said in a way that sounded too tired to be bothering.

She reached forwards for it, but he pulled it back out of her reach.

"But, like, there's no point if you can't pay for it."

Shona stopped reaching for it.

Tino saw that and smiled.

"But, hey, I can sort that too. Look, I'm not old enough to sign the contract on it, but there's this guy, we call him Pops, and he can sort this too. All he needs is for you to come by... You know, for ... er ... security."

Was he talking total lies? Shona looked at him fully in the face.

No, it seemed possible.

By now the line had moved so Shona reached the counter: she ordered two bags of chips – and there was no money left.

Tino leaned in. "Is that all you're having?" he asked.

Shona didn't answer. She hated this. She hated it, hated it, hated it. That's right, she didn't have any more money, and that's why she wasn't buying the fishcake to go with it, which she would have loved to have bought if she could.

"And?" said Tino as he put a tenner on the counter.

Maria was waiting; the till was open.

"Just say it. Sheesh, you're so dumb," Tino butted in.

She couldn't stop herself. She looked at the golden fishcakes on the rack and saw herself biting into it, through the crispy outer layer into the sweet flavours inside.

"Fishcake!" she blurted.

Tino handed Maria the cash, shrugged like

Shona was just his irritating little sister who had tagged along.

"Can I get the thing done now?" Shona asked.

"Sure," said Tino, "it's not me holding things up."

"I've got to get these chips to my dad first. We're in that block behind the shops."

"Yeah, sure. We'll see you here in ten," and Shona saw him wink at Gazz.

In a way, Shona felt kind of proud that she had done what needed to be done to get this phone. Others might have given up. After all, she had met up with these older boys when, *I bet,* she thought, people like Serena wouldn't have. But then, wasn't it like what Nan said, you have to take risks if you want to survive? OK, this wasn't about surviving, more about having something that she really, really had to have, but it was *like* surviving.

Tino and Gazz stopped in doorway of the old

block of flats by the garage and pressed a button.

"Delivery?" a voice said through the little speaker.

"Delivery," Tino answered.

Delivery? thought Shona. *We're not delivering anything.* As the security door clicked open, she looked at Tino with a puzzled look.

"Yeah," said Tino, "it's a joke thing we do. Like I'm the delivery guy."

"Yeah," said Gazz, "we always do that," and he laughed.

Upstairs, there was another security door outside the ordinary door and Shona could hear a dog.

Gazz put his fingers in his mouth and whistled. The dog stopped. Then, the inner door opened, followed by a heavy, barred security door and they went in. A thick, musky smell caught her throat, and she noticed that the walls had once been made to look cool, in the way nightclubs look on TV, but the place was dirty and now there was a hole in the ceiling.

Tino and Gazz were more up on their toes than

before, and Shona could hear them both breathing faster and louder.

They went down an unlit passage to a sitting room, and she could see that there were four more boys and a man sitting in a chair that was too big for him. He was tanned and his teeth showed up against his neatly trimmed beard.

They all touched fists and nodded, while Tino namechecked Shona to Pops, and Pops back to Shona.

Pops smiled, smoothing down his trousers as he spoke. *His shirt's too tight*, Shona thought, *it's like his belly is trying to escape*. "Thank you so much for helping out with that package the other day. We're all in so much of a hurry these days, aren't we?"

He seems to speak in a posher way than people round here, Shona thought, looking at his shiny shirt rather than straight into his face.

This seemed to cause a bit of a laugh, which Shona didn't understand, and for what was really the first time in this whole endless business of trying to get the phone, she felt now that maybe it wasn't worth it. This was a totally creepy sort of a place and she shouldn't be here. She made a move as if to step back, but it was spotted straight away by Pops.

"No, no, no, young lady, take no notice of them. Boys, eh?" He pulled a face to say they were all dumb and she and him knew that, even if they didn't know it themselves. He pushed a bowl of chocolates towards her.

"These are nice," he said, "believe me."

Shona took one. He was right. It was more than nice.

"Look, we can sort this contract out, right now. All I need from you is your signature," he said.

While she put her name on a piece of paper which she didn't read (and even if she had, was pretty certain that she wouldn't understand), Pops said in a quiet voice, in a casual, throwaway tone, "Anyone else who hasn't got a phone amongst your mates?"

He reached forward to the glass table in front of him and served himself an olive.

"No," said Shona, "no, they've all got phones. Oh no, hang on … maybe Serena. I haven't seen her with one…"

"Ah," he said, glancing at Tino. "Look, I can't promise her a freebie like yours – you did us a big favour the other day, that's why yours comes for nothing – but this Selina, if you could see to it, that you find out if she needs a phone, I'll see what I can do."

"Coming over," shouted Tino, and he threw the phone towards Shona.

For a moment it was like a drone, its black metal and glass reflecting back the light as it flew through the air. She wasn't ready for it and was sure that she'd clutch at it and miss – but no! Her hands were in the right place at the right time and she caught it.

A tiny wave of appreciation flowed towards her, but she didn't acknowledge it.

"Hey, Tino," said Pops, "she's good." He turned back to Shona and, seeing her unease and itchiness to get away, said, "No need to hang about here with us lot. Who would, eh? But Tino will be in touch about your mate Selina."

"It's Serena," Shona said.

"You are very good. You're on it."

Yes, I am, thought Shona. *I am right on it. I've got a phone that's cost me nothing, and I've got a connection that's cost me nothing too.*

"Gazz!" Pops flicked his fingers, and that seemed to be a command for Gazz to see Shona out.

It's like they obey orders from this Pops, Shona thought as she walked back through the street, tapping on her phone with her thumb like someone with a twitch in her hand.

He had scarcely washed himself, and made everything tidy, by emptying the basin out of the window, agreeably to the Jew's directions, when the Dodger returned, accompanied by a very sprightly young friend, whom Oliver had seen smoking on the previous night, and who was now formally introduced to him as Charley Bates. The four sat down, to breakfast, on the coffee, and some hot rolls and ham which the Dodger had brought home in the crown of his hat.

"Well," said the Jew, glancing slyly at Oliver, and addressing himself to the Dodger, "I hope you've been at work this morning, my dears?"

"Hard," replied the Dodger.

"As nails," added Charley Bates.

"Good boys, good boys!" said the Jew. "What have you got, Dodger?"

"A couple of pocketbooks," replied that young gentleman.

"Lined?" inquired the Jew, with eagerness.

"Pretty well," replied the Dodger, producing two pocketbooks; one green, and the other red.

"Not so heavy as they might be," said the Jew, after looking at the insides carefully; "but very neat and nicely made. Ingenious workman, ain't he, Oliver?"

"Very indeed, sir," said Oliver. At which Bates laughed uproariously; very much to the amazement of Oliver, who saw nothing to laugh at, in anything that had passed.

"And what have you got, my dear?" said Fagin to Bates.

"Wipes," he replied; at the same time

The Dodger said nothing, but he smoothed Oliver's hair over his eyes, and said he'd know better, by and by; upon which the old gentleman, observing Oliver's colour mounting, changed the subject by asking whether there had been much of a crowd at the execution that morning? This made him wonder more and more; for it was plain from the replies of the two boys that they had both been there; and Oliver naturally wondered how they could possibly have found time to be so very industrious.

When the breakfast was cleared away; the merry old gentleman and the two boys played at a very curious and uncommon game, which was performed in this way. The merry old gentleman, placing a snuffbox in one pocket of his trousers, a notecase in the other, and a watch in his waistcoat pocket, with a guard chain round his neck, and sticking a mock diamond pin in his shirt: buttoned his coat tight round him, and putting his spectacle case and handkerchief in his pockets, trotted up and down the room with a stick, in imitation of the manner in which old gentlemen walk about the streets any hour in the day. Sometimes he stopped at the fireplace, and sometimes at the door, making believe that he was staring with all his might into shop windows. At such times, he would look constantly round him, for fear of thieves, and would keep slapping all his pockets in turn, to see that he hadn't lost anything, in such a very funny and natural manner, that Oliver laughed till the tears ran down his face. All this time, the two boys followed him closely about: getting out of his sight, so nimbly, every time he turned round, that it was impossible to follow their motions. At last, the Dodger trod upon his toes, or ran upon his boot accidentally, while Charley Bates stumbled up against him behind; and in that one moment they took

from him, with the most extraordinary rapidity, snuffbox, notecase, watch guard, chain, shirt pin, pocket handkerchief, even the spectacle case. If the old gentleman felt a hand in any one of his pockets, he cried out where it was; and then the game began all over again.

When this game had been played a great many times, a couple of young ladies called to see the young gentleman; one of whom was named Bet, and the other Nancy. They wore a good deal of hair, not very neatly turned up behind, and were rather untidy about the shoes and stockings. They were not exactly pretty, perhaps; but they had a great deal of colour in their faces, and looked quite stout and hearty. Being remarkably free and agreeable in their manners, Oliver thought them very nice girls indeed. As there is no doubt they were.

The visitors stopped a long time. Spirits

were produced, in consequence of one of the young ladies complaining of a coldness in her inside; and the conversation took a very convivial and improving turn. At length, Charley Bates expressed his opinion that it was time to pad the hoof. This, it occurred to Oliver, must be French for going out; for directly afterwards, the Dodger, and Charley, and the two young ladies, went away together, having been kindly furnished by the amiable old Jew with money to spend.

"There, my dear," said Fagin. "That's a pleasant life, isn't it? They have gone out for the day."

"Have they done work, sir?" inquired Oliver.

"Yes," said the Jew; "that is, unless they should unexpectedly come across any, when they are out; and they won't neglect it, if they do, my dear, depend upon it. Make 'em your models, my dear. Make 'em your models," tapping the fire shovel on the hearth to add force to his words; "do everything they bid you, and take their advice in all matters - especially the Dodger's, my dear. He'll be a great man himself, and will make you one too, if you take pattern by him. Is my handkerchief hanging out of my pocket, my dear?" said the Jew, stopping short.

"Yes, sir," said Oliver.

"See if you can take it out, without my feeling it; as you saw them do, when we were at play this morning."

Oliver held up the bottom of the pocket with one hand, as he had seen the Dodger hold it, and drew the handkerchief lightly out of it with the other.

"Is it gone?" cried the Jew.

"Here it is, sir," said Oliver, showing it in his hand.

"You're a clever boy, my dear," said the playful old gentleman, patting Oliver on the

Chapter 11

By now, Shona had worked out that the place to be at break and lunchtimes was "The Wall". Yeah, most boys went off to a place lower down where they ran about like dogs chasing a ball, but now she knew everyone and everyone knew her, The Wall was best. Some sat on it, others leaned against it; they weren't allowed to walk on the top of it, in case they fell off it and died instantly, but sitting was OK. Shona stood talking to Désol'é about how she had once had fried chicken from the place on the Broadway and it tasted like sick, but all the time she was talking she was checking out Serena.

Serena, Serena, Serena.

It felt like Serena was a target and Shona was throwing a dart at it. Shona had run through in her mind how it was going to work: she'd be next to Serena, she'd get out her phone, read a message, laugh, and then reply to it. She'd put it back in her pocket and say, "Hey, I haven't got your number."

Then, the idea was, Serena would say, "I haven't got a phone"; Shona would say, "I can get you one"; and that would sort it.

Désol'é had moved on to talking about science homework and whether the next test was going to be about climate or not. At the same time, Shona strained to catch what Serena was saying in her place by The Wall as she chatted to Rasheda. Was she talking about the climate homework too?

Désol'é was asking her something.

"Yeah," said Shona, not really sure what she was saying yes to... Just then, Shona noticed something. Serena's jacket was torn. There was a tear at the back, down on one side. Not a big tear, just a little "L" of a tear. Did Serena know? If she did know, then why was she wearing the jacket?

Something about this tear triggered off a chain of thoughts in Shona's mind, to do with the jacket, and money to buy jackets, and money to buy phones, money to pay for using phones, and how it seemed so weird that she – and maybe Serena, maybe others – scraped around for money to pay for things, and others – like Harry and Sunil – seemed to have whatever they wanted. "Is it two hydrogen atoms and one oxygen atom, or the other way round? I can't remember which one the 'two' is about!"

Why did Désol'é think that Shona would know? Why was she asking her? Or was Désol'é doing it to help her? Just pretending she needed help, so that Shona would try to remember the science for the test. If so, that was kind.

"I think the hydrogen is two and the oxygen is one," Shona said, more guessing than remembering, and thinking of Serena the target, hit with a dart. *Why am I doing this? Just because they got me a phone doesn't mean that I have to hook Serena into this.* But then, but then, thinking of "hooking" and being "hooked", she thought, *Why am I hooked?* Her mind flashed back to that D8 when all it was about was this boy giving her a phone, which was great, but now it was all about getting Serena hooked in, and she was doing a favour for that Pops guy sitting in his flat with those boys, like Gazz and the rest, doing little sly laughs.

She felt the phone in her pocket. It was so great to have it. Maybe Serena would think like that ... longing to have a phone just like she had, and then feeling so great to have one.

But still there was that nagging thing going on in her mind about these boys and the Pops guy. *I mean, I get a phone just because I did them that favour with the package from the shop? Really? Maybe there's something else going on and I'm not getting it.*

I'm not getting it. Her mind finally came to a stop on: *I'm not getting it. I'm not getting it.* Désol'é was asking her about evaporation. She was being kind. She could see it in her face. Désol'é was getting her to revise right there by The Wall.

"Do you get it?" Désol'é asked.

"No, not really," Shona said and Désol'é took it to mean that Shona hadn't got how evaporation causes cooling, but Shona was somewhere else.

Désol'é tried to explain once again how a surface that water evaporates FROM, is what cools, yeah, and Shona gripped her phone and said to herself that until she did get what Tino, Gazz, Pops and the others were all doing, then she wouldn't and shouldn't get Serena in on this too.

And then, even as she made up her mind, and even as she gripped her phone, she had the thought that if she didn't "deliver" Serena, then couldn't Pops decide to not pay for the connection? Yes, he could, she answered herself, he can do what he wants, him in his little beard, and his belly fighting to get out of his shirt, and his "Have a chocolate, young lady" or whatever. "Go on, then," Désol'é said.

"Evaporation causes cooling," Shona blurted, summoning the words up from somewhere they must have stuck, without knowing they had, "and that means the surface that ... er ... the water evaporates FROM..."

"Go on..."

"Cools?" said Shona; her voice made a question mark in the air.

"YES!" shouted Désol'é, demanding high fives from Shona.

The bell went, and Désol'é thought, *and high fives to me for doing exactly what Miss Cavani asked me to do for Shona.*

CLASS X10 READING COMPREHENSION

At length, one morning, Oliver obtained the permission he had so eagerly sought. There had been no handkerchiefs to work upon, for two or three days, and the dinners had been rather meagre. Perhaps these were reasons for the old gentleman's giving his assent; but he told Oliver he might go, and placed him under the joint guardianship of Charley Bates and his friend the Dodger.

The three boys sallied out; the Dodger with his coat sleeves tucked up, and his hat cocked, as usual; Bates sauntering along with his hands in his pockets; and Oliver between them, wondering where they were going, and what kind of manufacture he would be instructed in first.

The pace at which they went was such a very lazy, ill-looking saunter that Oliver soon began to think his companions were going to deceive the old gentleman, by not going to work at all. The Dodger had a vicious tendency, too, of pulling the caps from the heads of small boys and tossing them down; while Charley Bates exhibited some very loose notions concerning the rights of property, by stealing apples and onions from the stalls at the kennel sides and thrusting them into pockets which were so surprisingly capacious that they seemed to undermine his whole suit of clothes in every direction. These things looked so bad that Oliver was on the point of declaring his intention of seeking his way back, in the best way he could; when his thoughts were suddenly directed into another channel, by a very mysterious change of behaviour on the part of the Dodger.

They were just emerging from a narrow

court not far from the open square in Clerkenwell, which is yet called, by some strange perversion of terms, "The Green": when the Dodger made a sudden stop; and, laying his finger on his lip, drew his companions back again, with the greatest caution and circumspection.

"What's the matter?" demanded Oliver.

"Hush!" replied the Dodger. "Do you see that old cove at the bookstall?"

"The old gentleman over the way?" said Oliver. "Yes, I see him."

"He'll do," said the Dodger.

"A prime plant," observed Master Charley Bates.

Oliver looked from one to the other, with the greatest surprise; but he was not permitted to make any inquiries, for the two boys walked stealthily across the road and slunk close behind the old gentleman towards whom his attention had been directed. Oliver walked a few paces after them, and, not knowing whether to advance or retire, stood looking on in silent amazement.

The old gentleman was a very respectable-looking personage, with a powdered head and gold spectacles. He was dressed in a bottle-green coat with a black velvet collar; wore white trousers; and carried a smart bamboo cane under his arm. He had taken up a book from the stall, and there he stood, reading away, as hard as if he were in his elbow chair, in his own study. It is very possible that he fancied himself there, indeed; for it was plain, from his abstraction, that he saw not the bookstall, nor the street, nor the boys, nor, in short, anything but the book itself: which he was reading straight through, turning over the leaf when he got to the bottom of a page, beginning at the top line of the next one, and going regularly on, with the greatest interest and eagerness.

What was Oliver's horror and alarm as he stood a few paces off, looking on with his eyelids as wide open as they would possibly go, to see the Dodger plunge his hand into the old gentleman's pocket, and draw from thence a handkerchief!

To see him hand the same to Charley Bates; and finally to behold them, both running away round the corner at full speed!

In an instant the whole mystery of the handkerchiefs, and the watches, and the jewels, and the Jew, rushed upon the boy's mind.

He stood for a moment, with the blood so tingling through all his veins from terror, that he felt as if he were in a burning fire; then, confused and frightened, he took to his heels; and, not knowing what he did, made off as fast as he could lay his feet to the ground.

This was all done in a minute's space. In the very instant when Oliver began to run, the old gentleman, putting his hand to his pocket, and missing his handkerchief, turned sharp round. Seeing the boy scudding away at such a rapid pace, he very naturally concluded him to be the culprit; and shouting "Stop thief!" with all his might, made off after him, book in hand.

But the old gentleman was not the only person who raised the hue-and-cry. The Dodger and Bates, unwilling to attract public attention by running down the open street, had merely retired into the very first doorway round the corner. They no sooner heard the cry, and saw Oliver running, than, guessing exactly how the matter stood, they began shouting "Stop thief!" too, and joined in the pursuit like good citizens.

Chapter 12

*A*s Shona pushed the door open to the rooms where she and Dad now lived, she felt for a moment she was pushing against everything that she had been thinking about: Serena, the phone, Pops and his flat, the looks on those boys' faces. What had seemed like a simple thing about getting a phone was now heavy and difficult. She would have asked Nan about it, but she could see that Nan was getting more and more touchy about her illness, like even walking round her stall was hurting her. Not much point in talking to Dad about it; he seemed to have given up.

If I had a mum, I'd tell her about it. Other kids at school came in talking about, "My mum says that I've got to do such-and-such", like it was some really bad thing to do with how they were not allowed to go to the caff on their own and how "unfair" it was to have a mum! *Yeah, really unfair. Try not having one.*

Dad was of course sitting on the sofa. Doing nothing. The door to her little box of a room was open and, looking past Dad into her room, she could see the edge of her picture of Mum. It was on the wall. That's funny; she hadn't put it there. She had left it on the chair next to her bed. Dad must have stuck it up there with something.

"Hi, kid," Dad said in a put-on American accent.

Shona ignored it, just grunted half-a-hello back and went into her room to dump her jacket on the bed. Nowhere else to put it.

"Ron put a hook on your door," Dad said.

"Who?"

"Ron," Dad said, "you know, the guy who brought our stuff over in his van."

"Who put this on the wall?"

"He had some sellotape."

"I didn't ask you to," Shona snapped back at him.

"I know…" he said, not knowing what to say next.

There was a pause. They couldn't see each other; Shona had half-shut her door.

"I'll take it down if you like."

"No point," Shona said. "It's up there, now."

She was staring at the photo and a shred of the old terror she got in the night floated past her, mocking her, jolting her, as if it was whispering, "You did that to me. You did that to me. That's why you haven't got a Mum. You brought all this on yourself."

It was enough to trigger the beginning of some crying. Shona turned away from the photo and came back into the main room. Dad was watching her and could see the tears in her eyes straight away.

He didn't know what to say. He didn't know what to do. Shona knew he didn't know what to say and do. He knew that Shona knew. They were both stuck in a hole with no way out.

"Like I said," Dad muttered, "I can take it down – it's only a bit of sticky tape. You know that stuff that Nan sells. It's rubbish, actually," he tried to laugh.

Shona paused. "It's OK, there. It's just that sometimes … sometimes I get scared."

Dad stared ahead of him. Shona noticed that "scared" seemed to ring a bell in his head.

"I know," he said.

He knew that she was scared by what she had done to Mum? *Does he really know that I think that?*

"Do you think I could have done more to save her?" Dad asked.

Shona looked at him. She suddenly realized that *he* was scared. He was scared that she thought he had done wrong, that it was all *his* fault that Mum hadn't lived.

The hole they were in was what both of them thought they had done to Mum. Shona was afraid to tell Dad, and Dad had been, up until this moment, afraid to ask her if she thought Mum's dying was his fault.

Shona thought about Dad's question. It had never occurred to her that he hadn't done enough. "No," she said, "you're not a doctor, are you?" It seemed a relief to him. Crazy! She was the one with the night terrors, and now she was comforting him.

They sat for a while. It was getting dark and neither of them had switched on the lights.

A slow realization crept over Dad: *Shona had said she was scared.* And he had said, "I know"; he did know, he knew the feeling. But thinking about that now, *What was Shona scared of? Ghosts?*

"Do you get the creeps with that picture by your bed, then?" he asked. "I mean, like it's a ghost or something?"

Shona screwed up her face. "No! As if!"

Dad was puzzled. Whatever could she be scared of, then? He didn't ask. They went on sitting in the dark.

Shona finally said it. Slowly and weakly, she said, "In the night, sometimes I think Mum is saying that I ... I did it."

"She says you did it?" Dad said, not believing that Shona could mean what he thought she meant.

She nodded, a single tear escaping down her cheek.

"No, no, no," Dad said, "of course you didn't. You were just a tiny thing. You just ... you just came into the world. It was wonderful. You did what you were made for. Swimming into the world."

He was crying too.

Shona leaned sideways on the sofa, and drooped like a sack against him. She hadn't hugged him and he hadn't hugged her for a long time. They had got to a point where they were like two cups at opposite ends of the table: in the same place, near to each other but not touching. He put his arm round her shoulder.

"I didn't realize," he said.

"I know," she said.

"And I really did do all I could," he said.

"Yeah," Shona said, "I know."

They sat together on the sofa, not saying anything more, each in wonder at not having had even a tiny sniff of a thought of how the other had been thinking, each in wonder that they had both had the same awful worries.

CLASS X10 READING COMPREHENSION

To refresh your memories, X10, Oliver had just taken off, chased by the gentleman at the bookstall (and Dodger and Bates). Oliver was caught and put to a rushed "trial" before a magistrate who was all too ready to sentence him when the bookseller arrived, out of breath, to declare himself a witness to Oliver's innocence. Oliver faints, and Mr Brownlow, the man who had been robbed, takes Oliver back to his own home to recover under the care of Mr Brownlow's housekeeper, Mrs Bedwin.

It had been bright day, for hours, when Oliver opened his eyes; he felt cheerful and happy. The crisis of the disease was safely past. He belonged to the world again.

In three days' time he was able to sit in an easy chair, well propped up with pillows; and, as he was still too weak to walk, Mrs Bedwin had him carried downstairs into the little housekeeper's room, which belonged to her. Having him set, here, by the fireside, the good old lady sat herself down too; and, being in a state of considerable delight at seeing him so much better, forthwith began to cry most violently.

"Never mind me, my dear," said the old lady; "I'm only having a regular good cry. There; it's all over now; and I'm quite comfortable."

"You're very, very kind to me, ma'am," said Oliver.

"Well, never you mind that, my dear," said the old lady; "that's got nothing to do with your broth; and it's full time you had it; for the doctor says Mr Brownlow may come in to see you this morning; and we must get up our best looks, because the better we look, the more he'll be pleased." And with this, the old lady applied herself to warming up, in a little saucepan, a basin full of broth: strong enough, Oliver thought, to furnish an ample dinner, when reduced to the regulation strength, for three hundred and fifty paupers.

"Are you fond of pictures, dear?" inquired the old lady, seeing that Oliver had fixed his eyes, most intently, on a portrait which hung against the wall; just opposite his chair.

"I don't quite know, ma'am," said Oliver, without taking his eyes from the canvas; "I have seen so few that I hardly know. What a beautiful, mild face that lady's is!"

"Ah!" said the old lady, "painters always make ladies out prettier than they are, or they wouldn't get any custom, child. The man who invented the machine for taking likenesses might have known that would never succeed; it's a deal too honest. A deal," said the old lady, laughing very heartily at her own acuteness.

"Is - is that a likeness, ma'am?" said Oliver.

"Yes," said the old lady, looking up for a moment from the broth; "that's a portrait."

"Whose, ma'am?" asked Oliver.

"Why, really, my dear, I don't know," answered the old lady in a good-humoured manner. "It's not a likeness of anybody that you or I know, I expect. It seems to strike your fancy, dear."

"It is so pretty," replied Oliver.

"Why, sure you're not afraid of it?" said the old lady: observing in great surprise, the look of awe with which the child regarded the painting.

"Oh, no, no," returned Oliver quickly; "but the eyes look so sorrowful; and where I sit, they seem fixed upon me. It makes my heart beat," added Oliver in a low voice, "as if it was alive, and wanted to speak to me, but couldn't."

"Lord save us!" exclaimed the old lady, starting; "don't talk in that way, child. You're weak and nervous after your illness. Let me wheel your chair round to the other side; and then you won't see it. There!" said the old lady, suiting the action to the word; "you don't see it now, at all events."

Oliver did see it in his mind's eye as distinctly as if he had not altered his position; but he thought it better not to worry the kind old lady; so he smiled gently when she looked at him; and Mrs Bedwin, satisfied that he felt more comfortable, salted and broke bits of toasted bread into the broth. Oliver had scarcely swallowed the last spoonful when there came a soft rap at the door.

"Come in," said the old lady; and in walked Mr Brownlow.

Now, the old gentleman came in as brisk as need be; he raised his spectacles on his forehead and thrust his hands behind the skirts of his dressing gown to take a good long look at the boy. Oliver looked very worn and shadowy from sickness, and made an ineffectual attempt to stand up, out of respect to his benefactor, which terminated in his sinking back into the chair again; and the fact is, if the truth must be told, that Mr Brownlow's heart, being large enough for any six ordinary old gentlemen, forced a supply of tears into his eyes.

"Poor boy, poor boy!" said Mr Brownlow, clearing his throat. "How do you feel, my dear?"

"Very happy, sir," replied Oliver. "And very grateful indeed, sir, for your goodness to me."

"Good boy," said Mr Brownlow, stoutly. "Have you given him any nourishment, Bedwin? Any slops, eh?"

"He has just had a basin of beautiful strong broth, sir," replied Mrs Bedwin: drawing herself up slightly, and laying strong emphasis on "broth": to intimate that between slops and broth there existed no affinity or connection whatsoever.

"Ugh!" said Mr Brownlow, with a slight shudder; "a couple of glasses of port wine would have done him a great deal more good. Wouldn't they, eh?"

The old gentleman looked in Oliver's face, the resemblance between his features and some familiar face came upon him so strongly, that he could not withdraw his gaze.

"I hope you are not angry with me, sir?"

said Oliver, raising his eyes beseechingly.

"No, no," replied the old gentleman. "Why! what's this? Bedwin, look there!"

As he spoke, he pointed hastily to the picture over Oliver's head, and then to the boy's face. There was its living copy. The eyes, the head, the mouth; every feature was the same. The expression was, for the instant, so precisely alike, that the minutest line seemed copied with startling accuracy!

Chapter 13

Désol'é and Shona were walking down one of the school's endless corridors. Some of Year 11's paintings were on the wall. Someone had done a perfect repro of *The Scream,* but there was a speech bubble coming out of the person's head, saying, "I can't find my lanyard..."

Désol'é looked sideways at Shona. "You all right?"

"Yep," Shona replied. She would never admit to *not* being all right to anyone.

"I'm meeting up with my cousin. She goes to Parkway and some of her squad are going to be there?"

"I can't," Shona said, "I've got one of these meeting things with Miss Cavani."

"Again? What number are you on now?"

"This is my sixth one," Shona said, nearly smiling.

"Next time," Désol'é said in a kind way and peeled off down another corridor while Shona walked on. And on.

Ahead of her, she could see some older boys. Not a good moment. She had already learned that it could be nasty if she was on her own when a bunch of boys walked past. There could be comments, there could be laughs, there could be a shove that pretended it wasn't a shove. Unless they were so wrapped up in something of their own, something massively important like Manchester United. Or Real Madrid.

The group got nearer, and in the middle of them, she recognized Gazz. He was shaking his head and flicking his hands, saying over and over again, "Man! No, I mean: man!"

He was stressed. No question of it, he was severely stressed. Not that the others in this group were helping him. If anything they were making it worse.

"Yeah," Shona heard one of them saying, "you ain't going to slip out of this one, Gazz, man."

"I know, I know, I KNOW!" Gazz shouted back at him. "Don't tell me what I know."

The others glanced at each other, doing cutting-throat signs, and finger-flicks. One of them was miming being on the phone and tapping out numbers.

As the group came up to and passed Shona, she heard Gazz blurt out, "They know where I am, even when I'm at my aunty's."

Was he crying? Shona thought he was. Not so cool now, like when he was Tino's mate, nodding and smiling at whatever Tino said. But then as the group moved on down the corridor behind her, this feeling drained away, and a worry rose to the surface: Gazz was part of how she had got her phone. He hadn't done much or said much, but he had been there all the time. The picture of what she had just seen stayed in her mind: Gazz shaking his head, the others doing cut-throat signs, but why the phone thing? Why was that boy doing a pretend dial-up?

Shona felt the phone in her pocket. She loved the

way she could feel its shininess with her fingertips. And then she remembered how she hadn't hooked Serena on to this free phone thing. It was as if her mind was being jerked to and fro between Gazz's stress, phones, Serena, and that scene at Pop's flat where it was all nicey-nicey but – come on! – it was a bit creepy, wasn't it?

The longer the corridor went on, the more uncomfortable Shona felt. The last picture on the wall of the corridor was a Year 11 painting of Michelangelo's statue of the Boy David, standing naked (of course) with the speech bubble above his head saying, "Sorry Miss, I left my homework on the bus."

Shona stared at the floor. She did like Miss Cavani, but not when she did her "investigating" thing. When she did that, it was like you were in the changing room at LQ Sports, and Miss Cavani had decided to get in there too, squashed up against you, asking you about what shampoo you used. Well, huh! Guess what, they were squashed in a little room, though Miss Cavani hadn't got on to any shampoo questions yet.

Miss Cavani was talking, and Shona was hearing, but not listening.

Shona lifted her head and looked at a series of pictures on the wall. An actor – or was she a dancer? – was in different poses with different faces: one moment hunched up and old, the next bold and upright, the next sad and mournful. It could almost be different people, but it really was the same person. Amazing. What would that feel like, where you didn't have to be yourself? One moment you'd be Shona and the next you could be Nan, the next you could be, well, Miss Cavani! Why not?

As Shona thought of how you could "be" Miss Cavani, the clasping and unclasping of the hands, the pushing back of the hair on the side of her head, Miss Cavani's words drifted in on Shona.

"...at a staff meeting and we've been alerted to the fact that..."

Why is she telling me this sort of stuff? Shona wondered.

"...warn you that an out-of-school gang operating..."

Hmm... Hmm... Shona felt irritated to see that the nail on her little finger had broken.

"...phones."

Shona heard that. Miss Cavani was talking about phones? And a gang?

"...hear of anything like that, not saying that you..."

It was like Désol'é trying to explain "evaporation". One moment it was a complete fog, then turned round the other way, it suddenly became clear. A gang? Phones?

Unlike "getting" evaporation, where she had felt relief she'd got it right, hearing what Miss Cavani was saying did just the opposite. Shona felt her stomach drop inside her. She wanted to gasp but stopped herself so as to not give anything away. It was like when you're in the pool and you're underwater and some idiot kid thinks it'd be really funny to push your head down and you feel panicky and breathless and water is rushing past your ears and eyes.

"…you've got a new phone, can I ask…"

No, no, don't tell her how. This is too big for Miss Cavani.

"My dad," Shona said quickly.

Miss Cavani looked closely at her. "I'll just say this, Shona dear. The way these things start always looks kind of nice. You know: generous. But it's much, much bigger than that. Things are taken, well, stolen, and passed along a line. The people taking the risks aren't really the ones making the money. It's people standing behind people. Things look like one thing but really they're another."

Miss Cavani leant forward, made to put her arm on Shona's shoulder – but stopped. She went on: "These people are always on the lookout for someone who can hand something on, keep things moving down the chain, get things sold, get the money moving around so that it all looks legal. Do you understand me?"

Shona "got" some of it, but not all of it. The bit that was "sticking" was the thing about "handing something on … getting things sold…"

"…now, I'm not going to go on about it any more…"

A picture came into Shona's head yet again: that time she was walking up to Nan's stall and there was that guy handing Nan a box and when the pair of them saw her, he slipped away like a fish in the water, and Nan started talking about something else. It was just a shifty moment. Nothing more. But somehow it chimed with what Miss Cavani was saying now.

Was it possible that Nan…? *Nan?!* She just ran a stall in the market. But then, what was it that Miss Cavani was saying about getting things moved on, sold? The picture of Nan's stall came to mind, and how one time she had gone to the caff to get Nan a cup of tea and when she came back, there was a row of hairdryers on the stall, all in their boxes. Just like that. A row of hairdryers. But how had Nan got them? Where did they come from?

But Nan, lovely Nan, who had hugged her tight, and looked after her so often...

Shona felt tears come into her eyes. It was all getting to be too much. Much too much.

CLASS X10 READING COMPREHENSION

Oliver was walking along on an errand for Mr Brownlow, thinking how happy and contented he ought to feel; when he was startled by a young woman screaming out very loud. "Oh, my dear brother!" And he had hardly looked up, to see what the matter was, when he was stopped by having a pair of arms thrown tight round his neck.

"Don't," cried Oliver, struggling. "Let go of me. Who is it? What are you stopping me for?"

The only reply to this was a great number of loud cries from the young woman who had embraced him; and who had a little basket and a street door key in her hand.

"Oh my gracious!" said the young woman, "I have found him! Oh! Oliver! Oliver! Oh you naughty boy, to make me suffer such distress on your account! Come home, dear, come. Oh, I've found him. Thank gracious goodness heavins, I've found him!"

With these incoherent exclamations, the young woman burst into another fit of crying, and got so dreadfully hysterical that a couple of women who came up at the moment asked a butcher's boy, who was also looking on, whether he didn't think he had better run for the doctor. To which, the butcher's boy: who appeared of a lounging, not to say lazy disposition: replied, that he thought not.

"Oh, no, no, never mind," said the young woman, grasping Oliver's hand; "I'm better now. Come home directly, you cruel boy! Come! He ran away, near a month ago, from his parents, who are hard-working and respectable people; and went and joined a set of thieves and bad characters; and almost broke his mother's heart."

"Young wretch!" said one woman.

"Go home, do, you little brute," said the other.

"I am not," replied Oliver, greatly

alarmed. "I don't know her. I haven't any sister, or father and mother either. I'm an orphan; I live at Pentonville."

"Only hear him, how he braves it out!" cried the young woman.

"Why, it's Nancy!" exclaimed Oliver; who now saw her face for the first time; and started back, in irrepressible astonishment.

"You see he knows me!" cried Nancy, appealing to the bystanders. "He can't help himself. Make him come home, there's good people, or he'll kill his dear mother and father, and break my heart!"

"What the devil's this?" said a man, bursting out of a beer shop, with a white dog at his heels; "young Oliver! Come home to your poor mother, you young dog! Come home directly."

"I don't belong to them. I don't know them. Help! Help!" cried Oliver, struggling in the man's powerful grasp.

"Help!" repeated the man. "Yes, I'll help

you, you young rascal! What books are these? You've been a stealing 'em, have you? Give 'em here." With these words, the man tore the volumes from his grasp, and struck him on the head.

"That's right!" cried a looker-on, from a garret window. "That's the only way of bringing him to his senses!"

"To be sure!" cried a sleepy-faced carpenter, casting an approving look at the garret window.

"It'll do him good!" said the two women.

"And he shall have it, too!" rejoined the man, administering another blow, and seizing Oliver by the collar. "Come on, you young villain! Here, Bull's-eye, mind him, boy! Mind him!"

Weak with recent illness; stupified by the blows and the suddenness of the attack; terrified by the fierce growling of the dog, and the brutality of the man; overpowered by the conviction of the bystanders that he really was the hardened little wretch he was described to be; what could one poor child do! Darkness had set in; it was a low neighbourhood; no help was near; resistance was useless. In another moment he was dragged into a labyrinth of dark narrow streets, and was forced along them at a pace which rendered the few cries he dared to give utterance to unintelligible. It did not matter, indeed, whether they were intelligible or not; for there was nobody to care, had they been ever so plain.

Chapter 14

Shona was running down the road. She didn't know what she was running from. Or what she was running to. Should she go home – huh, home! – or go and see Nan and ask her what was going on? Or what?

In amongst all her worries about being in trouble, there was also the feeling that she had been so stupid. So, so, so stupid. If only you could get hold of all those feelings and bundle them all into a bag and stuff them in a wheelie bin. One of those big ones that ran alongside the market. The market – yes, go and see Nan and just sort it. Yes, Nan would know how to do that.

The air was full of a damp mist, that wasn't rain and wasn't fog. Just a cold wetness that hung in the air.

She headed for the market, round by the Lennox Lewis estate, and slipped into the shortcut alleyway that ran past the old people's sheltered housing. That's when she heard something. Ahead of her, where the alleyway turned sharp right and sharp left, she heard some voices, scuffling sounds and a cry.

She froze. She knew the sound of a fight. She had heard it before. Once when she was in the Infants there had been a fight outside her school when Nan had come to pick her up, and Nan had bustled her away from it. And now, come to think of it … Nan had known their names! At the time it didn't seem strange, but now … it fitted.

Shona stopped stock-still. She couldn't see anything; whatever was happening was going on round the corner in the alleyway. She started to back up very slowly and silently away from the noise when she heard a voice she recognized:

"I didn't," the voice said, and there was more scuffling, the sound of thuds, and the same voice cried out.

Who was it? She knew that voice. Yes, it was Gazz! Was he being beaten up?

Standing stock-still, she heard another voice: it was deeper, muttering, and she couldn't make out the words, but again, it was another voice she recognized. Who, though? Who? She couldn't stop herself from straining to hear, even though the best thing to have done at this moment was run, get out of there, get out of everything, wash it all off, get away.

Who was this second voice?

And again, she got it. It was *Ron*, the man who had helped them move. Lugging stuff up and down the stairs.

Shona turned and ran back down the alley, and as she burst out on to the pavement, she ran into a man and a woman, dressed in uniform, with bits of high-vis attached, their pockets swollen with stuff.

"Sorry, love," said the woman, stepping to one side.

Shona looked at her. That rang a bell. The policewoman who had stepped to one side as she had been going through the tunnel in school … and hadn't she seen her before? In the market, and had heard Nan say "Specials".

The woman looked again at Shona, and said, "Shona! You OK?"

Her head was buzzing with everything that had happened and everything she had thought in the last few hours, and it felt like a can of drink that fizzes out the moment you pull back the ring. She looked from the woman to the alley behind her, and back to the woman and then without even thinking about it, pointed towards the bend in the alley. "There!" she said in a loud whisper, "there!"

There was something in the way that Shona said that word that clicked with the Specials woman. It was the sound of panic and fear in Shona's voice, and without waiting another second, she and the other policeman started running towards the bend in the alley.

Shona knew that she didn't want to – shouldn't – *couldn't* – hang about. This was all getting too fearsome, too dangerous. She ran towards the market to see Nan.

As she reached the busy end at the oranges stall, she looked beyond it to Nan's stall and could see in a blink of the eye that it was empty. It was all set up, but nothing on it, and no one behind it.

No Nan. Shona had wanted to sit down with her, ask her what it was all about, what was going on, what should she do? But now, nothing. Just not there.

She pushed her way into the caff and tried to catch Zeynep's attention. For the moment, Zeynep was busy with a customer who was saying that he asked for tea without milk and didn't want to drink this stuff and then as Zeynep came back to the counter, she saw Shona.

Shona didn't have to ask her.

"This morning, love," Zeynep said. "The ambulance came. She's in the Fenster." She put her hand on Shona's arm and shook her head.

Shona knew what this all added up to, and ahead of her, in her mind, she could see a huge, dangerous space: a nothingness where there was no Nan.

Somehow she had to get to the Fenster and see Nan. Someone had to help her.

We'll skip ahead, Class X10, to further in the book for the next reading. Oliver at this point has been stolen away by Nancy and the man, whose name was Bill Sikes. He was a brutal criminal, a real tough character, and the pair returned Oliver to Fagin's base. There he was kept prisoner, so he couldn't say anything to the police about Fagin and his crew. It wasn't long before Fagin and Sikes started planning a house robbery in the countryside, with another criminal named Toby Crackit. But they needed someone small, who could fit through a window.

They needed Oliver, of course.

They had cleared the town, as the church bell struck two.

Quickening their pace, they turned up a road upon the left hand. After walking about a quarter of a mile, they stopped before a detached house surrounded by a wall: to the top of which, Toby Crackit, scarcely pausing to take breath, climbed in a twinkling.

"The boy next," said Toby. "Hoist him up; I'll catch hold of him."

Before Oliver had time to look round, Sikes had caught him under the arms; and in three or four seconds he and Toby were lying on the grass on the other side. Sikes followed directly. And they stole cautiously towards the house.

And now, for the first time, Oliver, well-nigh mad with grief and terror, saw that housebreaking and robbery, if not murder, were the reason for the expedition. He clasped his hands together, and involuntarily uttered a subdued exclamation of horror. A mist came before his eyes; the cold sweat stood upon his ashy face; his limbs failed him; and he sank upon his knees.

"Get up!" murmured Sikes, trembling with rage, and drawing the pistol from his pocket; "Get up, or I'll strew your brains upon the grass."

"Oh! for God's sake let me go!" cried Oliver. "Let me run away and die in the fields. I will never come near London; never, never! Oh! pray have mercy on me, and do not make me steal. For the love of all the bright angels that rest in Heaven, have mercy upon me!"

The man to whom this appeal was made swore a dreadful oath, and had cocked the pistol, when Toby, striking it from his grasp, placed his hand upon the boy's mouth, and dragged him to the house.

"Hush!" cried the man; "Say another word, and I'll do your business myself with a crack on the head. That makes no noise, and is quite as certain. Here, Bill, wrench the shutter open. He's game enough now, I'll engage. I've seen older hands of his age took the same way, for a minute or two, on a cold night."

Sikes, cursing Fagin for sending Oliver on such an errand, plied the crowbar vigorously, but with little noise. After some delay, and some assistance from Toby, the shutter to which he had referred, swung open on its hinges.

It was a little lattice window, about five feet and a half above the ground, at the back of the house: which belonged to a scullery at the end of the passage. The opening was so small that the residents had probably not thought it worthwhile to cover it more securely; but it was large enough to admit a boy of Oliver's size, nevertheless.

"Now listen, you young limb," whispered Sikes, drawing a dark lantern from his pocket and throwing the glare full on Oliver's face, "I'm a going to put you through there. Take this light; go softly up the steps straight afore you, and along the little hall, to the street door; unfasten it, and let us in."

"There's a bolt at the top you won't be

able to reach," interposed Toby. "Stand upon one of the hall chairs. There are three there."

"Keep quiet, can't you?" replied Sikes, with a threatening look. "The room door is open, is it?"

"Wide," replied Toby, after peeping in to satisfy himself. "The game of that is, that they always leave it open with a catch, so that the dog, who's got a bed in here, may walk up and down the passage when he feels wakeful. Ha! Ha! Barney 'ticed him away tonight. So neat!"

Although Mr Crackit spoke in a scarcely audible whisper, and laughed without noise, Sikes imperiously commanded him to be silent, and to get to work. Toby complied, by first producing his lantern, and placing it on the ground; then by planting himself firmly with his head against the wall beneath the window, and his hands upon his knees, so as to make a step of his back.

This was no sooner done, than Sikes, mounting upon him, put Oliver gently through the window with his feet first; and, without leaving hold of his collar, planted him safely on the floor inside.

"Take this lantern," said Sikes, looking into the room. "You see the stairs afore you?"

Oliver, more dead than alive, gasped out, "Yes."

Sikes, pointing to the street door with the pistol barrel, briefly advised him to take notice that he was within shot all the way; and that if he faltered, he would fall dead that instant.

"It's done in a minute," said Sikes, in the same low whisper. "Directly I leave go of you, do your work. Hark!"

"What's that?" whispered the other man.

They listened intently.

"Nothing," said Sikes, releasing his hold of Oliver. "Now!"

In the short time he had had to collect his senses, the boy had firmly resolved that, whether he died in the attempt or not, he would make one effort to dart upstairs from the hall, and alarm the family. Filled with this idea, he advanced at once, but stealthily.

"Come back!" suddenly cried Sikes aloud. "Back! Back!"

Scared by the sudden breaking of the dead stillness of the place, and by a loud cry which followed it, Oliver let his lantern fall, and knew not whether to advance or fly.

The cry was repeated - a light appeared - a vision of two terrified half-dressed men at the top of the stairs swam before his eyes - a flash - a loud noise - a smoke - a crash somewhere, but where he knew not - and he staggered back.

Sikes had disappeared for an instant; but he was up again, and had him by the collar before the smoke had cleared away. He fired his own pistol after the men, who were already retreating; and dragged the boy up.

"Clasp your arm tighter," said Sikes, as he drew him through the window. "Give me a shawl here. They've hit him. Quick! How the boy bleeds!"

Then came the loud ringing of a bell, mingled with the noise of firearms, and the shouts of men, and the sensation of being carried over uneven ground at a rapid pace. And then, the noises grew confused in the distance; and a cold deadly feeling crept over the boy's heart; and he saw or heard no more.

Chapter 15

"I've got to see her," Shona said to Zeynep.

"Of course. Of course, dear," Zeynep said, "but the Fenster is two bus rides from here. You can't go on your own, and you don't know which ward she's in. They won't just let you wander round the hospital looking for her."

Shona had been ready to dash off, but what Zeynep said had slowed her to a standstill. She slumped down at an empty table, still with a couple of plates with a few chips and splashes of ketchup on them. After all that running and worrying, she felt her arms and legs suddenly go slow and heavy.

"I'll bring you a hot milk, and we'll work out how you can get down there. Just stay put, dear."

Shona did "stay put". She couldn't have done anything else for the time being. Far off, she heard a police siren. Or was it an ambulance? Or a fire engine? And then another. A feeble sun shone on the window as if it was struggling to get into the caff, but gave up at the door. Zeynep was ferrying kebabs, chips and sausages.

The door opened, and in stepped the "Specials" woman, still bulked up with her swollen pockets and high-vis jacket. She caught sight of Shona and sat down opposite her at the table.

"I'm Ashley," she said.

Shona didn't say anything.

"Did you know that boy they were roughing up?"

Shona didn't say anything.

Zeynep came over. "I think…" she began, with an edge in her voice.

"I'm not questioning her," Ashley said. "I know her. Shona, isn't it? I'm just having a chat."

She is *questioning me*, Shona thought. Zeynep moved off to collect a chicken-and-chips from the counter.

"Tell you what. I'm breaking every rule in the book here. But listen. You know Gazz and Tino, don't you? Your number's on Gazz's phone. Look, I've said too much already, but we think you know Pops. Somewhere down the line, you're going to have to tell us what you know. I know your situation, Shona."

These were words Shona had heard before: "your situation". She knew exactly what they meant: no Mum, Dad feeble. And now she could add "Nan ill" to the list of the "situation". And all this stuff about phones, and Tino and Gazz and Pops. It was all the "situation". And Ashley knew all this? Well, she was always hanging around, just as Nan had said.

Shona heard herself breathing fast. It was hopeless. And she was helpless. She couldn't even get herself to see Nan. And of course Dad couldn't help either.

She started crying.

"Hey, c'mon," Ashley said in a tough-but-kind way.

Zeynep came over. She had been "earwigging" as Nan would have said, listening in to what Ashley and Shona were saying. "Her nan's in the Fenster," Zeynep said and opened her eyes wide.

Ashley got the message. "You mean she's been taken in?"

Zeynep nodded.

"OK, OK, I'm off duty at five. I'll run you there."

Shona couldn't believe it. Was it really that easy? One moment Nan seemed to be a hundred miles away, and now she was just "over there", "nearby", a "few minutes in the car".

Zeynep went back to the counter and brought back a cheese sandwich. "I found this," she said, winking at Ashley and handing it to Shona.

Shona looked up at Zeynep, though Zeynep was swimming through Shona's watery eyes. All the same Shona smiled gratefully at her.

Ashley got up. "I'll be back," she said and as she moved off, she added, "Yolanda Cavani is one of the good guys, you know."

And she was off.

Miss Cavani? She knew Miss Cavani? Why not? Shona'd seen Ashley in the tunnel that time. And that didn't mean that was the only place she visited!

The car bobbed through the traffic, while Adele sang to them through the speakers.

"I love her," Ashley said. "She is so real. This one, listen to this one. People will be singing that for the next fifty years, believe me. The thing is, she knows what she's singing about. It's not made up, you get me?"

Shona nodded and listened in. It meant she didn't have to listen to her own thoughts.

"Your nan was on Gazz's phone as well," Ashley said quietly but just loud enough to pull Shona in.

But Shona said nothing. For a moment she felt

like a bit of chicken on one of Zeynep's skewers: well and truly caught. And yet … yet … had she, Shona, done anything wrong? It felt like she had, and yet she hadn't, had she? She had a phone. Was that against the law? Well, she supposed, it can't actually be a "free" phone, can it? It must have been nicked. And I've got it. And … I'll have to give it back.

She could just see the way Ashley might say, "And can I see your phone, Shona dear?" and it would slip out of sight into one of Ashley's swollen pockets.

A woman in a huge, high black car hooted behind them.

"Tractor coming through!" Ashley called out.

Shona looked puzzled.

"It's what I call them," Ashley laughed. "We're jam-packed here, waiting for the lights to change, and there's always some hoity-toity driver trying to shove their way through, like we're sheep in the way on a farm track. You ever been to the country, Shona?"

"Yes," Shona said, "on a school trip. We stayed

on a farm and had to clean up the manure and a man came and told us a story. It's his farm, I think."

"Hmm..." Ashley said, "what was the story about?"

"A giant iron man," Shona said. She remembered it well. That stay at the farm was the best time she ever had at primary school. Even cleaning up the manure!

"And if you could go on holiday anywhere in the world, where would you go?" Ashley asked her.

Little Shona Walker, sitting on a saucer...

That day on the beach she was crying! And the woman who brought her an ice cream came into her mind.

"A beach," Shona said.

"But where?" Ashley asked her again.

And for some reason she didn't even know herself, she said, "New York."

Ashley flicked the car indicator.

"New York? Is there a beach in New York?"

Shona felt silly and ignorant and said nothing. She didn't know if there was a beach in New York or not. She didn't know anything about New York, apart from what she had seen on TV. And yet there she was saying that the beach she wanted to go to should be there? *Where did that come from?* she wondered.

Eventually Ashley swerved into a car park, jumped out, slamming the doors, and then hurried across the car park to the Fenster.

Shona hung back at reception while Ashley talked with the woman. Their voices went quieter and without saying anything, Ashley guided Shona over to the lift.

The way their voices went quiet had put a chill down Shona's back. It was the kind of quiet-voice sound that means bad news, Shona knew. You don't have to ask, you just pick it up from the air.

The lift was huge and empty, big enough to carry a car, but it was only them in it. They didn't say anything and Ashley kept her eyes away from Shona. On the fourth floor, again, she guided Shona out and down a corridor. Another corridor. Always corridors. Going on and on and on.

They turned into Galsworthy Ward and Ashley went over to one of the nurses. More quiet talking. Very quiet talking and then all three of them walked past some beds with bottles and machines all around them, till they stopped by one just the same, bottles and machines. In it lay Nan, small, grey and still.

The nurse called out, "Your granddaughter is here to see you, Mrs Venner. Your granddaughter. Shona!"

Everyone knows my name, Shona thought, and the nurse walked away.

Nan's eyes opened no more than a hair's breadth. Just enough to see Shona. And just enough to see Ashley. The eyelids closed again. *It's like she's shrunk, poor thing,* Shona thought.

Then from out of the smallness came a tiny whisper. Shona couldn't catch what Nan said.

"I can't hear you, Nan," she said and leant in closer.

"Stay out of it," Nan whispered. "Stay out of it. It's not worth it."

The effort to say it made her tired; her mouth closed and there was no more movement.

Shona and Ashley sat by the bed, doing nothing.

Nan whispered, "Lorraine knew it."

And again, her mouth closed and there was no more movement.

This time, Ashley stepped forward, looked closely and then stepped further forward and pulled a cord.

The nurse came as fast as she could without

actually running, and stepped up to the bedside. She put two fingers on Nan's neck, and glanced at Ashley, and with no more than the slightest nod indicated to her that she should take Shona away.

Very, very gently, Ashley put her arm across Shona's shoulder and moved her away, out of the room and on to some chairs at the edge of the ward.

They sat down without saying anything.

"Best that way," Ashley said.

Shona looked at the floor. Is that it? What's "best" about it?

They sat for some more in quiet.

"A year ago, I was there when my dad went," Ashley said, and as she spoke her voice trembled. "He was Irish. The last thing he said to me was, 'Big eejit!' It's what he called himself. You never forget the last things they say."

Shona stared at the floor. She could just see herself in the shine of the surface. A shadowy blur.

What was it that Lorraine knew?

Did you think Oliver had died? No, Class X10, he hadn't. He had been left behind by the robbers and taken in by the woman living in the very house they had been trying to force Oliver to help them rob! Can you imagine that, helping someone like that, who had just very nearly robbed you?

Well, the woman living there – Rose Maylie was her name – came to believe Oliver's story, and she grew very fond of him as he recovered.

Meanwhile, Nancy worked out where Oliver was staying, but instead of telling Fagin and Sikes, she kept the information to herself, out of pity for poor Oliver who finally had a chance to avoid a life of poverty and crime.

But then, when a mysterious man came to see Fagin asking about Oliver, she realized she had to do something.

"Tell me why you wished to see me. I am the person you inquired for," said Rose.

The kind tone of this answer, the sweet voice, the gentle manner, the absence of any haughtiness or displeasure, took the other girl completely by surprise, and she burst into tears.

"Oh, lady, lady!" she said, clasping her hands passionately before her face, "if there was more like you, there would be fewer like me - there would - there would!"

"Sit down," said Rose, earnestly.

"Let me stand, lady," said the girl, still weeping, "It is growing late. Is - is - that door shut?"

"Yes," said Rose, recoiling a few steps, as if to be nearer assistance in case she should require it. "Why?"

"Because," said the girl, "I am about to put my life and the lives of others in your hands. I am the girl who dragged little Oliver back to old Fagin's on the night he went out from the house in Pentonville."

"You!" said Rose Maylie.

"I, lady!" replied the girl. "I am the infamous creature you have heard of, that lives among the thieves, and that never from the first moment I can recollect my eyes and senses opening on London streets have known any better life, or kinder words than they have given me, so help me God! Do not mind shrinking openly from me, lady. I am younger than you would think, to look at me, but I am well used to it. Thank Heaven upon your knees, dear lady, that you had friends to care for and keep you in your childhood, and that you were never in the midst of cold and hunger, and riot and drunkenness, and – and – something worse than all – as I have been from my cradle. I may use the word, for the alley and the gutter were mine, as they will be my deathbed."

"I pity you!" said Rose, in a broken voice. "It wrings my heart to hear you!"

"Heaven bless you for your goodness!" rejoined the girl. "If you knew what I am sometimes, you would pity me, indeed. But I have stolen away from those who would surely murder me, if they knew I had been here, to tell you what I have overheard. Do you know a man named Monks?"

"No," said Rose.

"He knows you," replied the girl; "and knew you were here, for it was by hearing him tell the place that I found you out."

"I never heard the name," said Rose.

"Then he goes by some other amongst us," rejoined the girl, "which I more than thought before. Some time ago, and soon after Oliver was put into your house on the night of the robbery, I - suspecting this man - listened to a conversation held between him and Fagin in the dark. I found out, from what I heard, that Monks - the man I asked you about, you know-"

"Yes," said Rose, "I understand."

"-That Monks," pursued the girl, "had seen him accidentally with two of our boys on the day we first lost him, and had known him directly to be the same child that he was watching for, though I couldn't make out why. A bargain was struck with Fagin, that if Oliver was got back he should have a certain sum; and he was to have more for making him a thief, which this Monks wanted for some purpose of his own."

"For what purpose?" asked Rose.

"He caught sight of my shadow on the wall as I listened, in the hope of finding out," said the girl; "and there are not many people besides me that could have got out of their way in time to escape discovery. But I did; and I saw him no more till last night."

"And what occurred then?"

"I'll tell you, lady. Last night he came again. Again they went upstairs, and I, wrapping myself up so that my shadow would not betray me, again listened at the door. The first words I heard Monks say were these: 'So the only proofs of the boy's identity lie at the bottom of the river, and the old hag that received them from the mother is rotting in her coffin.'

They laughed, and talked of his success in doing this; and Monks, talking on about the boy, and getting very wild, said that though he had got the young devil's money safely now, he'd rather have had it the other way; for, what a game it would have been to have brought down the boast of the father's will, by driving him through every jail in town, and then hauling him up for some capital felony which Fagin could easily manage, after having made a good profit of him besides."

"What is all this!" said Rose.

"The truth, lady, though it comes from my lips," replied the girl. "Then, he said, with oaths common enough in my ears, but strange to yours, that if he could gratify his hatred by taking the boy's life without bringing his own neck in danger, he would; but, as he couldn't, he'd be upon the watch to meet him at every turn in life; and if he took advantage of his birth and history, he might harm him yet. 'In short, Fagin,' he says, 'you never laid such snares as I'll contrive for my young brother, Oliver.'"

"His brother!" exclaimed Rose.

"Those were his words," said Nancy, glancing uneasily round, as she had scarcely ceased to do, since she began to speak. "And more. When he spoke of you, and said it seemed contrived by Heaven, or the devil, against him, that Oliver should come into your hands, he laughed, and said there was some comfort in that too, for how many thousands and hundreds of thousands of pounds would you not give, if you had them, to know who your two-legged spaniel was."

"You do not mean," said Rose, turning very pale, "to tell me that this was said in earnest?"

"He spoke in hard and angry earnest, if a man ever did," replied the girl, shaking her head. "He is an earnest man when his hatred is up. I know many who do worse things; but I'd rather listen to them all a dozen times, than to that Monks once. It is growing late, and I have to reach home without suspicion of having been on such an errand as this. I must get back quickly."

Chapter 16

Miss Cavani staggered into the room with a large, flat board. She propped it up at the front, clapped her hands and smiled. The buzz of chat slowed and stopped.

Shona sat quietly next to Désol'é. She had told Désol'é some of what had happened: the bits that she felt OK about telling her. Dad said that she could bring Désol'é to the funeral if she wanted to. She was beginning to think that she would like that ... if she knew how to ask her.

"On the other side of this board," Miss Cavani said, "is a picture."

For some reason, that got Crayton and Rory glancing at each other and smirking. *What world do we live in, where all you have to say is a word like "picture" and that gets them going?* Shona thought.

"I want you to look at it – say nothing, just look at it – and I want you to imagine that you are the person in the middle of that picture. You'll know which person that is when I turn the board round. Please remember one thing, X10. There are one or two people in this school – perhaps you know them, perhaps you don't – who have seen things like this in real life. It happens."

X10 went quiet. Miss Cavani turned the board. It was a painting of what immediately struck them all as an awful scene. A row of men with rifles were taking aim at a man whose arms were in the air, with a terrible look on his face.

"I want you to think of words, phrases, thoughts – anything that describes to you how you think that person feels. Just keep it to yourself for the moment.

No need to write it down, just say those words over
and over to yourself."

The room was quiet and people looked at the
picture. Shona felt the horror in the man's eyes and
could almost feel herself lifting her arms to imitate
what the man was doing, as if he was hanging
from a clothes line. In a second, he would be gone.
Finished. All over. And he knew that. Terror. But
he's pleading. The last thing he'll ever do in his life
is plead to stay alive. Terror and pleading.

After about thirty seconds, Miss Cavani said, "That's great, X10. Respect. I'm not going to ask you to share those thoughts with us just for the moment. We're going to read the next scene from *Oliver Twist*. Maybe – I don't know for sure – but some of the words that you thought might be thoughts you'll have as we read this scene. When we're through, what we're going to do is make our own paintings by doing 'freeze frames'. You know the deal. We create a picture of one of the moments in the scene. As we're reading, think about what moment you'd like to choose. We'll do it in pairs today, I think… Let's go. Oh hang on, who's going to read … ermm…" Miss Cavani's eyes looked round the room. "Noah, he's the charity boy – the bully. He's now come to London and joined Fagin's gang. Now, who's going to play him?"

"I will!" said Rory.

"Shona ought to do that one, miss," said Crayton, lifting his fists to his own face.

Shona saw what he was doing there and even gave a bit of a smile.

Miss Cavani looked down at the cast list again.

Shona called out, "Well, I'll do Nancy!"

"That's great, that's really great, Shona! Thank you!" And Miss Cavani meant it.

Harry wanted in. "I'll do Bill Sikes, miss!"

"Yeah, I bet you will…" Sunil said, with a wink across to Crayton.

That caught Harry off guard, and a blush crept up his neck.

"Right! Let's do it," said Miss Cavani.

CLASS X10 READING COMPREHENSION

"Wot d'ye mean?" asked Sikes, drawing back.

Fagin made no answer, but bending over the sleeper again, hauled him into a sitting posture. When his assumed name had been repeated several times, Noah rubbed his eyes, and, giving a heavy yawn, looked sleepily about him.

"Tell me that again - once again, just

275

for him to hear," said the Jew, pointing to Sikes as he spoke.

"Tell yer what?" asked the sleepy Noah, shaking himself pettishly.

"That about Nancy," said Fagin, clutching Sikes by the wrist, as if to prevent his leaving the house before he had heard enough. "You followed her?"

"Yes."

"To London Bridge?"

"Yes."

"Where she met two people."

"So she did."

"A gentleman and a lady that she had gone to of her own accord before, who asked her to give up all her pals, and Monks first, which she did – and to describe him, which she did – and to tell her what house it was that we meet at, and go to, which she did – and where it could be best watched from, which she did – and what time the people went there, which she did. She did all this. She told it all every word without a threat, without a murmur – she did – did she not?" cried Fagin, half-mad with fury.

"All right," replied Noah, scratching his head. "That's just what it was!"

"What did they say, about last Sunday?"

"About last Sunday!" replied Noah, considering. "Why I told yer that before."

"Again. Tell it again!" cried Fagin, tightening his grasp on Sikes, and brandishing his other hand aloft, as the foam flew from his lips.

"They asked her," said Noah, who, as he grew more wakeful, seemed to have a dawning perception of who Sikes was, "they asked her why she didn't come last Sunday, as she promised. She said she couldn't."

"Why – why? Tell him that."

"Because she was forcibly kept at home by Bill, the man she had told them of before," replied Noah.

"What more of him?" cried Fagin. "What more of the man she had told them of before? Tell him that, tell him that."

"Why, that she couldn't very easily get out of doors unless he knew where she was going to," said Noah, "and so the first time she went to see the lady, she - ha! ha! ha! it made me laugh when she said it, that it did - she gave him a drink of laudanum."

"Hell's fire!" cried Sikes, breaking fiercely from the Jew. "Let me go!" Flinging the old man from him, he rushed from the room, and darted, wildly and furiously, up the stairs.

"Bill, Bill!" cried Fagin, following him hastily. "A word. Only a word."

The word would not have been exchanged, but that the housebreaker was unable to open the door: on which he was expending fruitless oaths and violence, when the Jew came panting up.

"Let me out," said Sikes. "Don't speak to me; it's not safe. Let me out, I say!"

"Hear me speak a word," rejoined Fagin, laying his hand upon the lock. "You won't be—"

"Well," replied the other.

"You won't be - too - violent, Bill?"

The day was breaking, and there was light enough for the men to see each other's faces. They exchanged one brief glance; there was a fire in the eyes of both, which could not be mistaken.

"I mean," said Fagin, showing that he felt all disguise was now useless, "not too violent for safety. Be crafty, Bill, and not too bold."

Sikes made no reply; but, pulling open the door, of which Fagin had turned the lock, dashed into the silent streets.

Without one pause, or moment's consideration; without once turning his head to the right or left, or raising his eyes to the sky, or lowering them to the ground, but looking straight before him with savage resolution: his teeth so tightly compressed that the strained jaw seemed starting through his skin; the robber held on his headlong course, nor muttered a word, nor relaxed a muscle, until he reached his own door. He opened it, softly, with a key; strode lightly up the stairs; and entering his own room, double-locked the door, and lifting a heavy table against it, drew back the curtain of the bed.

The girl was lying, half-dressed, upon it. He had roused her from her sleep, for she raised herself with a hurried and startled look.

"Get up!" said the man.

"It is you, Bill!" said the girl, with an expression of pleasure at his return.

"It is," was the reply. "Get up."

There was a candle burning, but the man hastily drew it from the candlestick, and hurled it under the grate. Seeing the faint light of early day without, the girl rose to undraw the curtain.

"Let it be," said Sikes, thrusting his hand before her. "There's enough light for wot I've got to do."

"Bill," said the girl, in the low voice of alarm, "why do you look like that at me!"

The robber sat regarding her, for a few seconds, with dilated nostrils and heaving breast; and then, grasping her by the head and throat, dragged her into the middle of the room, and looking once towards the door, placed his heavy hand upon her mouth.

"Bill, Bill!" gasped the girl, wrestling with the strength of mortal fear, "I - I won't scream or cry - not once - hear me - speak to me - tell me what I have done!"

"You know, you she devil!" returned the robber, suppressing his breath. "You were watched tonight; every word you said was heard."

"Then spare my life for the love of

Heaven, as I spared yours," rejoined the girl, clinging to him. "Bill, dear Bill, you cannot have the heart to kill me. Oh! Think of all I have given up, only this one night, for you. You shall have time to think, and save yourself this crime; I will not loose my hold, you cannot throw me off. Bill, Bill, for dear God's sake, for your own, for mine, stop before you spill my blood! I have been true to you, upon my guilty soul I have!"

The man struggled violently, to release his arms; but those of the girl were clasped round his, and tear her as he would, he could not tear them away.

"Bill," cried the girl, striving to lay her head upon his breast, "the gentleman and that dear lady told me tonight of a home in some foreign country where I could end my days in solitude and peace. Let me see them again, and beg them, on my knees, to show the same mercy and goodness to you;

and let us both leave this dreadful place, and far apart lead better lives, and forget how we have lived, except in prayers, and never see each other more. It is never too late to repent. They told me so - I feel it now - but we must have time - a little, little time!"

The housebreaker freed one arm, and grasped his pistol. The certainty of immediate detection if he fired flashed across his mind even in the midst of his fury; and he beat it twice with all the force he could summon, upon the upturned face that almost touched his own.

She staggered and fell: nearly blinded with the blood that rained down from a deep gash in her forehead; but raising herself, with difficulty, on her knees, drew from her bosom a white handkerchief - Rose Maylie's own - and holding it up, in her folded hands, as high towards Heaven as her feeble strength would allow, breathed one prayer for mercy to her Maker.

It was a ghastly figure to look upon. The murderer staggering backward to the wall, and shutting out the sight with his hand, seized a heavy club and struck her down.

Miss Cavani looked round.

"I've said 'Respect!' once already to you, guys, I'm going to say it again. Well done to you all. You know I don't usually pick anyone out for special treatment. Today, I'm going to make an exception. Shona, that was … that was … *extraordinary*."

Almost before Miss Cavani finished saying this, the class applauded. They clapped. She was right, they thought, it had been amazing. She had been Nancy. She had lived it in her voice and even – if anyone glanced at her in her movements – even as she sat in her place in class. Something had clicked – some kind of switch, was it? – and it had enabled Shona to capture what had happened to Nancy and make it reach everyone else.

Miss Cavani set up everyone in pairs to do their "freeze frames". Maybe it was the way it was written, or maybe the way Shona had performed the words, maybe it was thinking about the terrible picture at the beginning of class, but everyone set about doing it. They chose different moments in the scene. No one played about.

They each had a chance to look at the poses they set up and talk about who they were and what they were doing. In a funny sort of a way, as they talked, as it flowed, the scene became more horrific, but less raw. The horror of what Sykes did became clearer, but they were now in a better place to think about it. Not just horror. But why Sykes did it, why Nancy said those things, why she clung to him, even though he was doing that to her. For the first time since she had moved to this school and settled in X10, Shona felt that she had "done" something. Like it worked. And that felt good.

What felt better was what happened later at the last session in the "suite". Miss Cavani said that at Christmas, they would be putting on a play version of another Dickens book. And she wanted Shona to audition to be Dickens.

What? How crazy was that? Really? Her?

"Yes, really," Miss Cavani said, and smoothed back the hair on the side of her head.

Chapter 17

Welcome to your final reading, X10. Oliver has gone on a long journey, from being born into a life of workhouse poverty to finding himself under the protection and care of Rose Maylie – and Mr Brownlow, the man who had been pickpocketed by Charley Bates and the Artful Dodger. Nancy, after she bravely helped Oliver, was killed by Bill Sykes, and a mob chased him through the streets; he ended up hanging himself during his attempt to escape. Here Oliver finally meets the mysterious man called Monks, who had claimed to be Oliver's brother! Let's see how this all wraps up – perhaps there is a twist?

At length, when nine o'clock had come, Mr Losberne and Mr Grimwig entered the room, followed by Mr Brownlow and a man whom Oliver almost shrieked with surprise to see; for they told him it was his brother.

Monks cast a look of hate at the astonished boy, and sat down near the door.

Mr Brownlow, who had papers in his hand, walked to a table near which Rose and Oliver were seated. "This is a painful task, but these declarations, which have been signed in London before many gentlemen, must be repeated here. This child," he said, drawing Oliver to him, and laying his hand upon his head, "is your half-brother; the illegitimate son of your father, my dear friend Edwin Leeford, by poor young Agnes Fleming, who died in giving him birth."

"Yes," said Monks, scowling at the trembling boy: the beating of whose heart he might have heard. "That is the bastard child."

"The term you use," said Mr Brownlow, sternly, "is a reproach to those long since passed beyond the feeble censure of the world. It reflects disgrace on no one living, except you who use it. Let that pass. He was born in this town."

"In the workhouse of this town," was the sullen reply. "You have the story there." He pointed impatiently to the papers as he spoke.

"I must have it here, too," said Mr Brownlow, looking round upon the listeners.

"Listen then! You!" returned Monks. "His father being taken ill at Rome, was joined by his wife, my mother, from whom he had been long separated, who went from Paris and took me with her - to look after his property, for what I know, for she had no great affection for him, nor he for her. He knew nothing of us, for his senses were gone, and he slumbered on till next day, when he died. Among the papers in his desk, were two, dated on the night his illness first came on, directed to yourself"; he addressed himself to Mr Brownlow; "and enclosed in a few short lines to you, with an intimation on the cover of the package that it was not to be forwarded till after he was dead. One of these papers was a letter to this girl Agnes; the other a will."

"What of the letter?" asked Mr Brownlow.

"The letter? A sheet of paper crossed and crossed again, with a penitent confession, and prayers to God to help her. He had palmed a tale on the girl that some secret mystery – to be explained one day – prevented his marrying her just then; and so she had gone on, trusting patiently to him, until she trusted too far, and lost what none could ever give her back. She was, at that time, within a few months of giving birth. He told her all he had meant to do, to hide her shame, if he had lived, and prayed her, if he died, not to curse his memory, or think the consequences of their sin would be visited on her or their young child; for all the guilt was his."

"The will," said Mr Brownlow, as Oliver's tears fell fast.

Monks was silent.

"The will," said Mr Brownlow, speaking for him, "was in the same spirit as the letter. He talked of miseries which his wife had brought upon him; of the rebellious disposition, vice, malice, and premature bad passions of you, his only son, who had been trained to hate him; and left you, and your mother, each an annuity of eight hundred pounds. The bulk of his property he divided into two equal portions - one for Agnes Fleming, and the other for their child, if it should be born alive, and ever come of age. If it were a girl, it was to inherit the money unconditionally; but if a boy, only on the stipulation that before he became an adult he should never have stained his name with any public act of dishonour, meanness, cowardice, or wrong. He did this, he said, to mark his confidence in the other, and his conviction that the child would share her gentle heart, and noble nature. If he were disappointed in this expectation, then the money was to come to you: for then, and not till then, when both children were equal, would he recognize your prior claim upon his purse, who had none upon his heart, but had, from an infant, repulsed him with coldness and aversion."

"My mother," said Monks, in a louder tone, "did what a woman should have done. She burnt this will. The letter never reached its destination; but that, and other proofs, she kept, in case they ever tried to lie away the blot. The girl had left her home, in secret, to hide her shame."

"I swore," said Monks, "if ever the child

crossed my path, to hunt it down; never to let it rest; to pursue it with the bitterest and most unrelenting animosity; to vent upon it the hatred that I deeply felt, and to spit upon the empty vaunt of that insulting will by draggin' it, if I could, to the very gallows-foot. She was right. He came in my way at last. I began well; and, but for babbling drabs, I would have finished as I began!"

As the villain folded his arms tight together, and muttered curses on himself in the impotence of baffled malice, Mr Brownlow turned to the terrified group beside him, and explained that the Jew, who had been his old accomplice and confidant, had a large reward for keeping Oliver ensnared: of which some part was to be given up, in the event of his being rescued: and that a dispute on this head had led to their visit to the country house for the purpose of identifying him.

"Young lady," said Mr Brownlow, turning to Rose, "give me your hand. Do not tremble. You need not fear to hear the few remaining words we have to say."

"If they have - I do not know how they can, but if they have - any reference to me," said Rose, "pray let me hear them at some other time. I have not strength or spirits now."

"Nay," returned the old gentleman, drawing her arm through his; "you have more strength than this, I am sure. Do you know this young lady, sir?"

"Yes," replied Monks.

"I never saw you before," said Rose faintly.

"I have seen you often," returned Monks.

"The father of the unhappy Agnes had two daughters," said Mr Brownlow. "What was the fate of the other - the young child?"

"The child," replied Monks, "when her

father died, the child was taken by some wretched cottagers, who reared it as their own."

"Go on," said Mr Brownlow, signing to Mrs Maylie to approach. "Go on!"

"You couldn't find the spot to which these people had gone," said Monks, "but where friendship fails, hatred will often force a way. My mother found it, after a year of cunning search - ay, and found the child."

"She took it, did she?"

"No. The people were poor and began to sicken - at least the man did; so she left it with them, giving them a small present of money which would not last long, and promised more, which she never meant to send. She didn't quite rely, however, on their discontent and poverty for the child's unhappiness, but told the history of the sister's shame, with such alterations as suited her; bade them take good heed of the child, for she came of bad blood; and told them she was illegitimate, and sure to go wrong at one time or other. The circumstances allowed for all this; the people believed it; and there the child dragged on an existence, miserable enough even to satisfy us, until a widow lady, residing, then, at Chester, saw the girl by chance, pitied her, and took her home. There was some cursed spell, I think, against us; for in spite of all our efforts she remained there and was happy. I lost sight of her, two or three years ago, and saw her no more until a few months back."

"Do you see her now?"

"Yes. Leaning on your arm."

"But not the less my niece," cried Mrs Maylie, folding the fainting girl in her arms; "not the less my dearest child. I would not lose her now, for all the treasures of the world. My sweet companion, my own dear girl!"

"The only friend I ever had," cried Rose, clinging to her. "The kindest, best of friends. My heart will burst. I cannot bear all this."

"You have suffered more, and have been, through all, the best and gentlest creature that ever shed happiness on everyone she knew," said Mrs Maylie, embracing her tenderly. "Come, come, my love, remember who this is who waits to clasp you in his arms, poor child! See here – look, look, my dear!"

"Not aunt," cried Oliver, throwing his arms about her neck; "I'll never call her aunt – sister, my own dear sister, that something taught my heart to love so dearly from the first! Rose, dear, darling Rose!"

Let the tears which fell, and the broken words which were exchanged in the long close embrace between the orphans, be sacred. A father, sister, and mother, were gained, and lost, in that one moment.

Joy and grief were mingled in the cup; but there were no bitter tears: for even grief itself arose so softened, and clothed in such sweet and tender recollections, that it became a solemn pleasure, and lost all character of pain.

A wind blew across the car park at the place everyone called "the Crem". Shona stood with Désol'é. People had turned up who she had never seen before, and as they came up to her they had said things like, "I'm your second cousin. Maybe your nan mentioned me." She hadn't. Or, "I was a friend of your mother's. Your nan was very good to me." And on it went.

Why had she never seen these people? It was like they were old, forgotten toys, and they had all come out of a cupboard, to say that they remembered this or that, and then in a few hours' time, they would all go back in the cupboard again. They even brushed down their black skirts and jackets like they had got dusty in there, as they waited quietly to come out and be played with one more time.

As they waited to go in, these toys moved into little groups and pairs, people who knew each other, standing together, shifting from foot to foot. People nodded from the safety of one group across the car park to another group. When another car turned up, or if someone strolled through the gates, Shona heard them say to each other, "Oh, here's Dave." Or, "Well I never, isn't that your uncle Vern?"

There was some scowling too. It didn't slip Shona's attention, even if she didn't know what old aggro, what old bitterness, lay behind the scowls.

But it was lovely to see Zeynep. They had closed the caff, she said, and she gave Shona a squeeze.

The service was slow, and the man got Nan's middle name wrong. He said it was Mary, but it was Maria. That annoyed Shona. It felt so bad that at this moment of all moments, the name was wrong, but then as he drew to a close and talked about Nan's stall, she felt a great well of tears from inside her and she cried and cried and cried while Désol'é held her tight. Dad was sitting on her other side, and she let him hold her hand. Or was she holding his hand?

As they drifted out into the wind, and people shook hands, someone mentioned the "Old Junk" which is what people round there called the Junction Tavern, and then someone else said that kids wouldn't be allowed in there, would they? But then a woman who hadn't really talked to anyone made a little move that made people turn their heads. She was tall, and walked like someone who had been taught to walk in that way. Maybe she had been a dancer? Actually, one or two people had wondered who she was but then as plenty of people there hadn't known each other, this woman hadn't grabbed too much attention. Up till now, that is.

"Excuse me," she said. "I don't want to interrupt. I know that people won't know who I am. And I know this is a strange time to be doing this, but … but…" The voice that had been strong before, did a little stumble. "But I'm Pam's sister."

There was total silence. Nan's sister?! One or two of the oldest ones smiled to each other, their memories going back thirty years or more to a girl they once met, who was now this woman, and they squeezed up their eyes to get a look at her. Others had no idea. Pam had a sister? Shona stared and stared at her. Nan had a sister? Did Nan ever mention her? She looked across at Dad, standing with Ron: his face was like the moon, white, staring, and still.

And just as Shona was running through things that Nan said, that might have been about this sister, the woman said in her strong voice:

"I'm Lorraine. I've arranged a little buffet in the place just along the road from here. The Athens. Please, come if you can. Please. And I'll explain everything there and not here in the wind."

Lorraine? Shona thought. The name that Nan had whispered! What was it she whispered about her? With so much going on it was so hard to remember everything. Shona looked as closely as she could at Lorraine's face. It seemed familiar: the smile. And the brown eyes.

Meanwhile, some of the people there were stunned. Some laughed.

Now, almost everyone started bundling off to the Athens, where there was indeed a lovely spread. One or two people knew Christo, the owner, and people started telling jokes – jokes about the weather, jokes about each other, jokes about Nan, jokes about one another's football teams.

Shona sat with Désol'é and a boy a bit older than her who had come up to her and said, "I think I'm a sort of cousin, or second cousin, or third cousin … but I don't know how…" and laughed.

At one point, Shona nipped off to the loo and, just as she was washing her hands, Lorraine came in.

"So, little Shona Walker, sitting in a saucer. I'm

your great-aunt," she said briskly.

Shona stared and stared and the moment on the beach came to her, the ice cream, when she was crying. And now she felt like crying again. It had been such a nice thing she had never ever forgotten … but why did she go away?

"Yes," said Shona, feeling a little as if she had been ambushed, but with a flutter inside that was telling her that, if anything as nice as that ice cream was going to happen, it was going to be good.

"At the moment, I know much more about you than you know about me. It may seem strange to you that I didn't show my face earlier. I had my reasons. Perhaps you can guess them. Your nan had her reasons for doing things too, and nothing anyone ever said to her could get her to stop. Let me say it like this: I figured that sometimes in life you have to steer clear of things, till it all gets a bit more sorted. It's why I went. I've been in New York."

Shona knew some of that already … it fitted. And Nan had said, "Lorraine knew that…" Lorraine knew it wasn't worth it, being part of the way Nan was.

Lorraine went on: "People have said I must be a hard-hearted body to have gone." She brushed her hair back from her face. "Not even got in touch with your father or you. It's not been easy."

She stared at herself in the mirror. Pouted her lips in the mirror and looked back at Shona.

"Your nan sent me a letter a few weeks ago, telling me everything. She knew how it was with the illness. I came back."

"When?" asked Shona.

"Ah. Well. Yes. A couple of weeks ago, so I got to see her. There's been a lot to arrange, as I'm thinking of coming back permanently. It seems to be the right time to come home. And hey, I can keep an eye on you, can't I?"

Shona smiled. It was the first time that someone saying they'd keep an eye on her sounded good.

"It's what your nan wanted. Me too. Things won't be so hard for you and your father as they have been. I promise you that."

Shona stared at her. For half a second, it reminded her of Pops, sitting in his chair so keen to do her a favour, offering her chocolates...The same thoughts seemed to have crossed Lorraine's mind. She laughed.

"No, no," she said, "I'm one hundred per cent. When I went over there, I had nothing. One contact. And then it was hard work, mind. But I'm not broke. I promise you, I'll do what I can for you and your father."

Shona stared at her. Was she saying that she was going to help them? She was. She was.

"You might have guessed something else: I haven't got any kids. No, don't worry, I'm not going to whisk you off pretending to be your mum. No, no, no. But I tell you what, can I be your friend?"

Shona smiled. In a way she already was. That ice cream on the beach had always been like a friend.

"And then, maybe further on down the line, I might become your auntie Lorraine. How about that? I'm your great-aunt, but I can still be 'auntie', right?"

Shona nodded carefully, trying not to smile this time because Lorraine was saying 'great-aunt' like it was "great ant".

"Now, here's a thing. How about I wrangle some tickets for something nice? And you bring your friend out there. She watches out for you, doesn't she?"

She does, Shona thought. The way Désol'é has been around, like, asking me to come to the canteen with her, and trying to help her with "Evaporation"! Evaporation, for goodness' sake. How crazy is that, thinking about "Evaporation" now?

Lorraine looked in the mirror, pouted her lips, and looked back at Shona.

"C'mon. Let's get back in there and see if we can cheer up that father of yours. It was quite a shock seeing him just then. He looks like someone pulled the plug out of his bathtub years ago and he can't find the tap to fill it."

Now that's funny, Shona thought. That is funny.

"C'mon. We can do this, Shona," Lorraine said to her.

And they walked out of the loo back into the Athens dining suite, where the music was already playing.

It was "Que Sera, Sera..."

Very loudly.

Michael Rosen

Michael is one of the best-known figures in the children's book world, renowned for his work as a poet, performer, broadcaster, professor, scriptwriter and author of classic books such as *We're Going on a Bear Hunt*. He was Children's Laureate from 2007–2009.

Tony Ross

After training at Liverpool School of Art, Tony worked as a cartoonist, graphic designer, advertising art director and art lecturer. Today he is best known for the *Horrid Henry* and *Little Princess* series of books, as well as illustrating books for David Walliams.

About Charles Dickens

Charles Dickens is one of the most famous English writers in history.

Born in Portsmouth in 1812, he is known for works such as *A Christmas Carol*, *Great Expectations*, *Bleak House* and *David Copperfield*. In 1837 he started publishing *Oliver Twist* in monthly instalments in *Bentley's Miscellany*, and readers of the magazine had to wait two years to find out how the story would end.

Dickens wrote the novel to criticize the harsh ways that poor people were treated at the time. He told the story of an orphan boy forced to live in a workhouse so that people could understand how difficult life was inside, and how few choices anybody living there had to improve their situation.

Oliver Twist has inspired many films, plays and musical adaptations over the years since it was first published. Although workhouses may have long since disappeared, readers can still relate to its message of compassion for others and its call for social justice.